Glitter

When Kate Maryon isn't writing, or walking her large Newfoundland dog, Ellie, or spending time with her grown-up children, Jane and Tim, or her grown-up stepchildren, Sam, Joe and Ben, or having fun with her husband Daniel, or visiting the rest of her family, or sitting in cafés and other lovely places with her friends, she can be found working from a clinic in Somerset, where she practises homeopathy, or in Devon where she works on detox retreats. And with all this going on there's never a shortage of stories and wonderful things to write about.

Kate loves chocolate, films, eating out, reading, writing and lying on sunny beaches. She dislikes snakes, spiders, peppermint and honey.

Also by Kate Maryon

Shine

A Million Angels

Glitter

Kate Maryon x

HarperCollins *Children's Books*

First published in Great Britain by HarperCollins *Children's Books* 2010
This edition published in 2011
HarperCollins *Children's Books* is a division of HarperCollins*Publishers* Ltd,
77-85 Fulham Palace Road, Hammersmith, London W6 8JB

The HarperCollins *Children's Books* website address is
www.harpercollins.co.uk

4

Glitter
Text copyright © Kate Maryon 2010

The author asserts the moral right to be identified as the author of this work.

ISBN-13 978-0-00-743318-6

Typeset in AGaramond by Palimpsest Book Production Limited,
Falkirk, Stirlingshire

Printed and bound in England by
Clays Ltd, St Ives plc

MIX
Paper from
responsible sources
FSC® C007454

FSC is a non-profit international organisation established to promote the
responsible management of the world's forests. Products carrying the FSC
label are independently certified to assure consumers that they come
from forests that are managed to meet the social, economic and
ecological needs of present and future generations.

Find out more about HarperCollins and the environment at
www.harpercollins.co.uk/green

For Daniel, Carole, Heather, Louisa, Ruth, James, Sophia, Mala and Joti, and for your mummies who now glitter with the stars in the sky – they loved you so much and were so sad to leave you.

For Jonny, Amida and all the other dads who did and continue to do their wonderful best.

For Jayne and Jan who will for ever glitter in my eyes – thank you for so much.

Chapter 1

Failure is not an option...

My dad is so obsessed with success that every time I'm home from school, for a weekend or for the holidays, he just can't resist reminding me of the Parfitt family motto.

"Remember, Liberty," he booms, while he's checking over my school work or reading my report, "that failure is not an option for a Parfitt." And what annoys me most is that he *always* says it as if I've never even heard it before. He *always* says it as if it's never been drummed into my head a thousand million times. He *always* says it as if I don't already know that I'm the biggest failure the Parfitt family has ever had the disappointment of knowing. And what makes things worse is that as hard as I try not to let his stupid motto bother me, it does. I just can't help it and every time he says it something deep inside me shrivels up and hides.

At my brother's parents' evening, his housemaster said to my dad, "Sebastian has a glittering career ahead of him, Mr Parfitt, he's a real credit to you, sir. He's brilliant at everything, an A* student from head to toe and there are top-secret whispers being passed around that he's going to be made next year's head boy."

You could almost see the gift-wrapped packages of love leaping out of my dad's heart and landing like glitter on my successful brother's smile.

My parents' evening wasn't quite so glittering. My dad had to cancel this extremely important business meeting to drive all the way from London, to our school in Somerset, where the news that hit his ears did not make him smile.

"She's a lovely girl, Mr Parfitt," my housemistress said, "kind, sweet and helpful, but she struggles with her academic studies. Liberty has more of a natural inclination towards her musical studies and I have to say she really appears to have a talent for it, sir. If she were to be encouraged a little more in this area she may well—"

"Music!" my dad blasted when the parents' evening was

over. "Music, Liberty! You're unbelievable! I made it perfectly clear to you when you were small how I felt about you pursuing an interest in music and the same remains today. It was music that ruined your mother's life and I won't have it ruin yours. My own mother was stupid enough to let me follow my dreams when I was at school and nothing good ever came of it. I should have listened to my father and gone into business from the start, that's where the security is, Liberty, you mark my words. But no, my dominating mother stuck her nose in and interfered as usual. So, I want you to listen to me good and listen to me hard. You will do as you're told and follow a sensible career, one that won't let you down or get you into trouble. You're going to be twelve years old soon and it's about time you put your head down and pulled your socks up. I don't pay a fortune in fees for you to be at one of the best schools in the country so you can mess about. I'm paying for you to get ahead in life and make something of yourself. I want to see an improvement, Liberty, and I want to see it fast. Do I make myself clear?"

"Yes, Daddy," I said, because I know there's never any point in arguing with him. He never listens to anything I have to say. Then he jumped in his car and roared off back to his office, without even saying goodbye. There was no little gift-wrapped parcel of love popping out of his heart for me; there never is. And that's all I want, really. I just want him to love me too and not just Sebastian. Or even just to like me one tiny little bit. That would be a start. But I only ever seem to make him angry which drives him further and further away.

Two weeks later at the end of year Prize-giving Day things went from bad to worse. Sebastian won six prizes and got to make his first speech as next year's head boy. And I got nothing! Zilch! Zero!

"I've had just about enough of this behaviour, Liberty," my dad fumed when we'd finished our special celebration lunch for Sebastian's success. "I'm shocked that you didn't even manage to pick up one prize. You're letting the side down, you know, giving us Parfitts a bad reputation and it really won't do. You have to start towing the line and soon."

I nodded and quietly tucked myself into the soft, red leather seats of his car. I tried to disappear and let his angry words drift over my head without letting them hurt me.

If only I'd known then, the truth about my dad and his own glittering success. If only I'd known the truth about what actually happened to my mum and the real fact that success has nothing to do with good marks or money, I might have found the courage to stand up to him and speak up. I might have found the words to say that I *would* win prizes, and lots of them, and that he could be proud of me and send me little parcels of love to land like glitter on my smile. And that I wouldn't be a failure and a disappointment to the Parfitt family, if only he'd just let me be who I am and follow my heart.

But I didn't know any of that then.

I just stared out of the window with the long summer holidays stretching out in front of me, with no idea of how much our lives were about to change.

Chapter 2

Humming might be dangerous...

My school is *amazing*. And I'm not lying. I mean, I know my dad does spend a small fortune on sending me there, but I truly think it's worth every penny. Being at boarding school is like being at one long, never-ending sleepover. I mean, of course, we have to do school work and stuff, but living with my friends all the time is so much better than living with my family. It's not as if I don't love Sebastian and my dad because I do. It's just, I feel lonely when I'm with them. If my mum were around things might be different, but something terrible happened to her when I was nine months old and she died. I don't remember anything about her and my dad refuses to tell me the kind of things I'd like to know. I have seen one photo of her so I know she had bright red, curly hair, just like mine. And I know she was obsessed with playing the violin, because my dad let it slip out one day, when he was getting stressed about me asking for violin lessons.

My dad has hated music ever since she died. He thinks it was the ruin of her but I don't understand how music could ruin your life. I think music is the most amazing thing that was ever invented. I mean, you don't even have to be clever or anything to love it. It's so simple. It can just dive into you and make your skin tingle and make the hairs on the back of your neck stand up on end and tickle you. It can make you feel happy or sad or excited or sleepy just like that, without even trying. And another thing I love about music is that you can hear a song or a piece of music and it can immediately take your mind back to a memory. Like the harvest festival song about the broad beans lying in their blankety beds. That one always takes me back to the time when Alice's mum took Alice and me to Disneyland Paris for the weekend. We just couldn't stop singing it, all the way in the car and in the plane. In fact we sang it so many times we started to drive Alice's mum so completely crazy that she bought us some lollipops just to make us shut up.

I don't sing when I'm around my dad. I have to zip my mouth. Even humming might be dangerous. Alice's mum bought me an iPod last Christmas and I downloaded all of my favourite pieces of music on to it. It's mostly violin music because that's my obsession and I'm not joking, I am truly obsessed with it. I think I must take after my mum. It's so easy to listen to because you can just imagine all of nature and the birds flying and the streams running and the sun shining. And it kind of moves like the wind through my hair and glitters like stars in the night and soars and dives and touches my skin like soft, gentle rain. When I'm home with my dad for the weekend I shut myself in my room and listen to my iPod in secret.

Being secret in our house isn't too difficult, because for a start it's enormous. We have eight bedrooms, although most of them aren't really used very often, and mine is at the top of the house. Our house is very tall and there are so many stairs up to my room that my dad's always too lazy to bother to come up and see me. But I wouldn't chance playing music that he might hear from his office – that would be too risky. Playing and listening to music might seem like a very strange thing for a girl not to be allowed to do and I agree it is. But my dad says he has his reasons and one day, I promise you, I'm going to get to the bottom of it all and find out the truth.

What I don't understand is why my dad cut us off from my mum's side of the family straight after her funeral. I mean, you might have thought it was an important thing to keep in contact with your family, but then my dad doesn't even have that much contact with his *own* mother, let alone someone else's. My dad is an only child and my grandpa died years ago because he was very old. So Granny is my dad's only surviving relative, apart from Sebastian and me, of course. My dad says that Granny is an interfering old battleaxe who needs to learn to keep her opinions to herself. I disagree; I think he should listen to her more, because sometimes she says things that I think make sense.

"What your father doesn't understand, Liberty," she said one day, "is that I inhabit the Wisdom of Age, not the Insanity of Youth."

On the few occasions in my life I've been brave enough to ask my dad about my mum he just sighed and said, "It's not helpful for any of us to be talking about your mother,

15

Liberty. Let the past stay buried in the past." Which is all very well for him, because it must be a terrible thing when your wife goes and dies, leaving you with two small children to take care of, but it's not very helpful if you're a curious type of person, like me.

I tried asking my granny the last time I went to stay with her. But she only had to look at me once with her shiny black eyes for me to know that questions about my mum are out of bounds. I do love my granny because, well, because she's my granny, but also because she takes me out for fun. We go on these amazing shopping trips and out for lunch and to the theatre and the ballet. I love the ballet, but we have to keep that secret from my dad.

"What we do in our time, Liberty," she says, "is our business and there's no need for your father to know any different."

When I go shopping with Granny it's always to Harrods. She thinks my dad is useless at buying the right kind of clothes for me, so twice a year she travels down from Scotland to take me out. I'm pretty much allowed to have what I like, so long as I have some sensible things like a warm coat and a special occasion dress and comfy shoes and things like that, as well. After shopping we always have tea at the Ritz. The Ritz is my granny's favourite place for tea and sometimes we have to meet her friends there too, which means I always get covered in bright red lipstick and half-choked to death with old ladies' perfume. And it means my manners have to be impeccable. Granny likes teaching me about manners and deportment and elocution because she says it's important for a young lady to be able to carry herself well in the world.

Even though our main house is in London, Granny always prefers us to stay in a hotel. She says that then my dad can't butt in on our fun.

Granny doesn't really understand about my obsession with the violin either. Whenever I try to talk to her about it she just coughs and changes the subject, then a little later she might whisper into my ear something like, "Never give up on your dream, Liberty, just keep it under wraps for now."

I think when she says things like that she is speaking from the Wisdom of Age. My dad has probably told her that the violin is a no go area for my life and for once she is listening to him and doing as he asks. I wish they would be friends; it would make Christmas and things like that much more fun. Granny always goes away for Christmas on a month-long cruise. She says that the winter sun is good for her constitution.

The first time I actually picked up a violin was when Alice and I both began boarding at our school. We were about seven years old and the moment she pulled it out of its case, I just knew I had to learn to play. The shiny chestnut wood and beautifully shaped bow and four little strings hypnotised me. I didn't even know anything about my mum and her violin obsession then; just the look of it, the feel of it and the sound of it were like wonderful magic to me and I couldn't take my eyes off of it or stop the thought of it dancing around my brain.

"Daddy," I said, on our first weekend home, "can I have violin lessons like Alice?"

"No, Liberty!" he shouted, so loud it made me jump out of my skin. "*I* am not wasting my money on music lessons and *you* are not to indulge an obsession like your mother's. Do I make myself clear? You'll learn what I want you to learn and do what I want you to do and that is that. End of story."

So I never asked again and Alice has never minded me borrowing *her* violin. We have our secret all worked out. Alice's mum pays for her to have the lessons and then Alice teaches me what she's learned. She isn't really interested in the violin, she's more of a bookworm and she only plays because her mum insists that it's an important addition to a young lady's list of accomplishments. Parents have very strange ideas sometimes. I'm not brilliant at it, but I can play quite well, especially for someone who's never had a proper lesson. Alice thinks I'm a natural. I wish, I wish, I wish I could play for my dad one day. Then he might see that I'm not such a total failure as he thinks and he might even start to love me just a little bit more. I truly think that if Alice were to ever leave our school and I couldn't play the violin any more, I really would just shrivel up and die.

Chapter 3

A glittering success...

"My summer was rubbish," I tell Alice while we're unpacking our trunks and settling back into school for the start of the autumn term. "My dad just dumped me in our French house for the whole ten weeks with strict instructions that I had to do at least four hours' school work every day. My granny wasn't well so he hired this scary dragon woman with whiskers on her chin to look after me and he didn't bother to come and see me, not even once. He kept phoning and saying he'd be over soon so we could go out on the boat. But he never even did. He just got more and more stressed and snappy on the phone as the weeks went by. Apparently something big was happening at work *again,* and he said it was too impossible to leave. Lucky Sebastian was off jet-skiing with a friend so I didn't get to see him either. Boring is an understatement, Alice. I had nothing to do but work, work, work, apart from the pool I suppose, but that's not much fun on your own. Sometimes I think my dad forgets I'm still a child."

"My summer was terrible too," sighs Alice, lying back on her bed. "My parents just bickered the whole time we were in Greece. I sometimes wonder why they even stay married. I mean, plenty of parents get a divorce. I don't know what the big deal is."

"Parents have strange ideas," I say. "I tried to talk to Sebastian about my mum and about what happened to her when we were out buying our uniforms. I wanted to see if there's an actual reason behind the fact that my dad won't let me play the violin. But he said he doesn't remember anything about her, except her red hair and a tune that she used to play to him while he was drifting off to sleep."

"That's so sad," says Alice. "I can't imagine what it would be like without my mum."

"I wish I could remember something about her," I say. "I wonder if she ever played a tune to me?"

When we've unpacked and had our tea and sat through a house meeting and shared summer stories and welcomed the new girls, Alice and I sneak out of our window and onto the flat roof to look at the sky. Above us is a soft glittering blanket that twinkles through the darkness and wraps us up in stars.

"I'm so glad to be back," I whisper.

"Me too," says Alice.

"Whoever invented the stars," I say, "truly was a glittering success. Can you imagine what it would be like to fly through them and feel them glittering all about you?"

"Of course a person didn't invent them, Libby," says Alice snuggling in close, "but imagine if they had. They would be the most popular and richest person in the world."

"No, Alice," I giggle, "your dad is the richest person in the world. Well, not like kings and princes, but he is rich."

"Your dad too," she says.

"I suppose so," I sigh. "It's just I don't really see the point of it when he's not happy and enjoying it. He's so moody and stressed all the time, who cares how much money he has? My dad wouldn't know how to enjoy himself if it came and bit him on the nose. That's what my granny says."

"Daddy says things are changing," whispers Alice. "He says the banks have more debts than they have money."

"What does that mean?" I ask.

"Don't know really," she shrugs. "He just says that things *will* change. But we don't need to worry about anything, Libby, nothing will happen to us, silly."

Having a best friend like Alice is as amazing as my school. I mean having a best friend, full stop, is brilliant, but for me it means I always have someone I can share my feelings with, someone I can trust. I know that whatever happens in our lives, Alice will be there for me and I will be there for her. That's how it is with us, it's simple. Alice is also very good at telling me the truth, even when it hurts.

"Can you try not to dump your feelings on me this term, Libby. We're nearly twelve and that's too old for lashing out."

"I'll try," I say. "It's just sometimes I can't help it. It must be my red hair."

"The colour of your hair is no excuse, Libby, you have to take responsibility for your feelings."

Chapter 4

Everything is really all my fault...

Three weeks later I'm sitting in a maths lesson with my mind half-drifting out of the window, when a prefect knocks on our door and tells our teacher that I have to go to the headmaster's office straight away. I am completely sure that I haven't done anything wrong or bad enough to need a trip to see Mr Jenkins, our headmaster, for a telling off, but anyway I'm careful to pull up my socks and straighten my tie before knocking on his door.

"Yes," booms his throaty voice, "come on in."

I turn the big brass handle, step inside and am surprised to see my dad sitting on one of Mr Jenkins's black leather chairs. He's looking all red-faced and flustered and

Sebastian is there as well, pacing about the room in tears. My heart dives into my tummy like a cold, hard pebble and bounces straight back up again and lodges in my throat.

"What's happened?" I ask, immediately leaping to the conclusion that somebody we know has died or that Sebastian only got a B for his science homework or something terrible like that.

"Come and sit down, Liberty," says Mr Jenkins. "I'm afraid your father has some rather upsetting news."

But I don't sit down. Because how can you sit down when the tension in the room is making you worried that your ears are about to hear some ultra-upsetting news? My dad looks terrible. He clearly hasn't shaved for a few days and he looks like he hasn't slept or eaten for weeks. I hover nearby without getting too close. I never know with my dad when he might unexpectedly bark some random command at me and make my feelings hurt. The headmaster coughs as a polite way of reminding my dad that it's his turn to speak now.

"Liberty, I'm afraid I have some bad news," whispers my dad, running his hand through his untidy hair. I'm shocked because I've never heard my dad speak so quietly before. His voice usually booms around the room, deafening my ears, but now he sounds like someone's just let the air out of him and there's nothing left for talking.

"The business has collapsed, Liberty," he says. "I've hung on for months and months, trying to keep it all going but now I've hit rock bottom, the official receiver has been called in and we've become victims of the credit crunch."

Then he looks at me like I know what all that means, which, of course, I don't. I mean I've heard of the credit crunch and everything and things closing down all over the place, because whoever on this planet hasn't? That was what Alice was saying her dad was talking about. He said things would change and he was right, but what has any of that got to do with me?

Then Sebastian explodes.

"What he's trying to say, Libby," he steams, "is that we've lost everything. And I mean, *everything*! All the houses, all the cars, the boat, all the shares and every last penny in the bank."

"Oh," I say, still not really understanding, but knowing that something has gone terribly wrong. "I'm sorry, Daddy." And suddenly it's like the word 'sorry' has been touched by the edge of a lit match and whooshed it up in flames.

"Sorry!" my dad bellows, full of air again. "What do you mean, 'Sorry'? Sorry is hardly going to help now, Liberty, is it? What are you talking about, child? It's far too late for sorry."

I flinch and begin to feel like the whole credit crunch thing and Dad's business collapsing and everything is really all my fault. All I want is to go back to my maths lesson, because right now maths feels like one hundred and fifty thousand times more interesting than the angry words that are flying out of people's mouths and around this room. Luckily Mr Jenkins takes charge.

"Liberty," he says, in a trying-to-explain-something-important-to-a-stupid-person kind of voice, "your father's here to take you home. He's come to pick you both up and take you home because he can no longer afford the fees to keep you here."

Dad makes whimpering, hurt dog sounds and his left leg keeps jiggling up and down like it can't stop.

"Home?" scoffs Sebastian. "And where exactly is that, Dad? Where is home?" And then he crumples in a heap on the floor, wiping his tear snot on his blazer sleeve. And my dad peers back at him through empty eyes. I'm afraid to even move an inch or say anything at all because I don't want to make anyone else shout. And I'm relieved when Mrs Peterson, the school secretary, arrives with a tray full of tea and biscuits. But Sebastian's not letting up and he turns on Mr Jenkins.

"After all I've done for this school," he shrieks, "and being head boy and everything. You can't just turf me out on the streets; I'm in my last year of A levels. This disaster might well ruin my whole life and I will hold you," he points to Mr Jenkins, "and you," he points to Dad, "personally responsible."

"Calm down, Sebastian," says Mr Jenkins, handing Sebastian a handkerchief and a cup of tea. "Of course I wouldn't just turf you out on the streets. At your stage in your education and with your brilliant academic record there are plenty of bursaries and charitable funds available to finance your last year with us. It's your father's decision to take you home."

Sebastian glares fury at Dad, wanting some answers.

"It's true, Seb," says Dad. "I can't help it; I'm a proud man. I owe the school the whole of last term's fees and there's no money left to clear the debt or pay for any more.

And that debt doesn't even touch the tip of the iceberg. I'm up to my neck in trouble, so I'm calling it a day. I've given it my best shot and now I'm drawing a line under it and we're moving on. Now, enough of this emotional display, I want the pair of you to go and pack your trunks immediately and we'll be off."

I don't think my mind is totally taking all of this information overload in, because my legs are definitely not making their way towards my dorm to pack my trunk. I'm just standing quietly, keeping my eyes on the ground, sipping on the hot tea and nibbling a chocolate biscuit, wondering if this is the last food I might be eating in a while, because of us having no money any more. And then Sebastian starts up again.

"I'm not leaving here, Dad," he spits, "and you can't make me. I'm nearly eighteen, so it's not like it's even your choice any more."

"Sebastian," Dad booms, finding his voice again, "you will do as I say. Now go and pack your trunk at once and meet me in the Grand Hall in fifteen minutes." Then he spins around and turns on me, making me jump and I spill a whole slop of tea in my saucer. "And that goes for you too, young lady. And I mean it, double quick sharp."

Chapter 5

I don't even know where to begin...

I slip out of Mr Jenkins's office and head towards my boarding house to pack my things. It's not until I'm passing the fountains in front of the dining room that the penny suddenly drops and I realise that my dad is here to take me home. But he can't take me home! What's he talking about? I've been boarding at this school since I was seven years old. This place practically *is* my home and everyone here is much more like my family than even my own dad is. I like it here; I don't want to go home. I wish I could run straight back to Mr Jenkins's office and tell my dad that he's got it all wrong. I wish I could beg Mr Jenkins to find some charitable something so that I can stay here, but my obedient legs keep on walking towards my room, afraid to stand up to my dad's shouting and angry face.

Matron is lurking outside my room, waiting for me and I can hardly even see her because I have angry, salty tears streaming down my face. She's already lugged my trunk from the trunk room and quickly starts helping me gather and fold my things. I keep dropping stuff because my whole insides have become trembling jelly and my teeth are chattering with cold, even though the warm autumn sun is shining through the open window. I pull my pony posters and cards and fairy lights from my pin board and fold my duvet and pillow into my trunk.

"Have you got time to go and say goodbye to everyone?" asks Matron.

I shake my head. "No, my dad's in a hurry and I don't even want to," I say, swallowing the lump in my throat. "I just want to disappear."

Just then, our dormitory door opens and Alice walks in. The bell for lunchtime must have gone off without me even noticing.

"What's happening, Liberty?" she asks. "What are you doing?"

I wish the floorboards would open up and swallow me

whole. Last year Bryony Eves was pulled out of school because her family ran out of money and the whole thing was so embarrassing for her. None of us were true friends, once she'd gone, we just forgot about her. I wonder where she is now?

"Matron will tell you," I say, pushing past her and heading for the door.

"But why is your trunk packed up, Libby? You can't just walk out and not tell me what's happening."

"I have to, Alice," I shout. Tears are prickling in the back of my eyes, threatening to flow over again. "I don't have any choice. I never have any choice. I have to go."

But Alice isn't going to be fobbed off. She knows me too well. She grabs me and makes me look at her.

"Liberty!" she shrieks. "Look at me; it's me, your best friend Alice here. Tell me what's going on."

"I have to leave the school, Alice, OK?" I shout. "Is that a good enough explanation for you?" And then I feel myself go, I feel the heat burning inside of me, filling my body with rage. "It's the credit crunch, Alice," I scream, throwing my washbag on the floor and trying to pull away from her. "Your dad was right about things changing and my dad's gone bust and now I'm like Bryony Eves. So go off to lunch and gossip about me, like we did her and then forget about me. Just get on with your own life, Alice, and forget I ever existed. I'm different now, I'm not part of this any more and I never will be, ever again. I have to go, my dad's waiting."

"Lashing out and throwing things isn't going to help, Liberty Parfitt," she says, gripping my arms. "I'm your friend, remember. I'm here for you whatever happens."

"Yes, well, that was then and now things have changed," I scream, yanking myself away from her and picking up my things. "And once I've gone you'll find a new friend to replace me. Now go back to school, Alice," I shout as I slam through the door, "and forget about me."

When I get back to the Grand Hall I find my dad sitting alone with his head in his hands, all of the air sucked out of him again. All my rage has been sucked out of me too and it's growing into cold goose bumps under my skin.

"Come on, Liberty," he sighs, "let's go."

"What about Sebastian?" I ask.

"He's convinced me to let him stay. Mr Jenkins is going to sort out some funding for him. He has so little time left here, even I can see the madness in taking him away. So it's just you and me, I'm afraid."

I want to scream again and ask if I can stay and get some funding too so I can stay at school. But deep down I know that screaming won't work, not with my dad, not with anyone. And anyway, I'm too scared to say anything because I can't bear to hear the truth. I'm not a success like Sebastian, I'm an embarrassment to the Parfitt family and nobody in their right mind would waste their precious funding money on me.

The porters carry my trunk out to the car park and help Dad tie it onto the roof rack of a rusty old banger that I have never even seen before. Matron appears, waving me goodbye and crying and tucking a copy of *100 Favourite Poems* into my hand. Mr Jenkins is shaking my other hand and wishing me good luck and good health for my future. And although I can hear all the good wishes coming from their mouths, I can't really feel them; they bounce off my blazer and fall like raindrops, splashing to the ground. Sebastian joins us, his eyes all red-rimmed and teary.

"Sorry, Libby," he says, pulling me into a hug. "I just have to stay... you know?"

"I know," I lie. "I'll be OK. And it's good for you stay.

It's important for your success. Don't worry about us, I'll take care of Dad."

"I knew you'd understand, sis, and I'll be home soon enough for the holidays," he promises.

"I'll miss you," I say, covering the scared wobble in my voice and climbing into the passenger seat next to Dad. "Have a good rest of term."

He gives my hand a friendly squeeze and keeps on waving us goodbye, until he's a tiny speck in the distance.

Our new car is noisy and smoky and travels at snail's pace compared to our old black Mercedes. The seats are battered and torn and big chunks of foam are forcing their way through the scratchy grey fabric. My dad sighs and turns on the Radio Four news to fill the awkward silence that is growing between us. The newsreader keeps groaning on and on about the credit crunch and financial scandals and I wish we could have something more cheerful, like music, to fill our car. But that will never be possible. After a while he huffs and turns the radio off. I feel lonely, like all the warmth and friendliness of my life at school has drained down the plughole and I'm left alone, sitting in an empty bath shivering, with no soft towel for comfort.

There's so much I want to ask, like what's happened to our houses and cars and where are we going to live and if he thinks that Sebastian really will come home for the holidays, because I don't think he will? But all of these questions are out of bounds because they might turn my dad into a snapping dog again. So I file them away in the back of my brain.

"Granny will help," I say. "I'm sure of it. Granny has the Wisdom of Age."

My dad's eyes flash fire at me. "I don't want you mentioning a word of this to your grandmother," he spits. "The last thing I need right now is for her to start interfering and busybodying around. Do you hear me, Liberty? I need you to keep your mouth firmly zipped. I need to find my own way out of this situation. And if I discover you two have been gossiping on the phone, there'll be trouble. OK?"

Chapter 6

Welcum to the dump...

My dad stops the car in front of a grey concrete block of flats somewhere in London.

"We're here, Liberty," he says. "I need you to help me with your trunk because it's not safe to leave it on the roof. It'll be gone in a flash."

"Where are we, Daddy?" I ask. "Who lives here?"

"We do," he says, running his hand through his hair, "for now anyway. I know it's a mess, Liberty, but this is what it's come to: a grotty flat in a grotty part of town."

"But why here?" I ask. "Why not home?"

"Because, as Sebastian so delicately put it, we don't actually have a home any more. He was right, Liberty; we don't have anything left. The bank has taken everything except a few personal bits. This flat belongs to a friend of mine, he usually rents it out, but it's free at the moment, so I moved in yesterday and we're staying here until I get back on my feet. It won't take long, I promise, I've got my finger in a few pies already."

I stare up at the ugly grey building.

"So we don't have a home?" I whisper.

Some big kids are click-clacking on skateboards, a few girls are playing hopscotch and there are some really young children squealing and running around playing catch without any grown-ups watching them. The words, "Welcum to the dump" are written in red graffiti on the wall near the lift. I've seen places like this on TV but I've never been to one in real life and I don't feel very welcome.

My trunk is heavy and it keeps twisting around and hurting my wrist. I try my hardest to be strong, but it's just too heavy for me. My dad sighs and ends up dragging it along on his own, while I manage our bags. He's not talking and when we discover the lift is broken, he groans and snaps while he bumps my trunk up the stairs. After we've gone up a couple of flights, he starts getting out of breath, so I try to help again. But he shakes me off, like I am an insect trying to bite him.

Beyond the green front door of our flat I find a few unfamiliar rooms to explore. A tiny kitchen with grey tiles, a sitting room with glass doors leading on to a balcony that has a few dead plants on it, a small bathroom and two bedrooms, one with a double bed and one with a single. I spy a pile of my things already heaped on the single bed and go on in to make myself at home. The room is tiny and has musty damp smells lurking in the corners. Whoever graffitied "Welcum to the dump" was right. It is. I try not to remember my beautiful bedroom in our London house, with my own en-suite bathroom and four-poster bed, or my room in our French house with its deep blue walls and wooden shutters that overlook the pool. A sick taste rises in my throat, which I swallow down fast.

I look out of my bedroom window onto the car park below. A sad lonely tree is crying autumn leaves that scatter in the breeze and I wish the wind would blow me back to school where I belong. I kick the stupid bed. It's small and tatty and old like the rest of this dump and I don't want to be here. I lie down and stare at the ceiling. It looks like it's made from a million tiny snowy mountains. I wish I were skiing on them. I close my eyes and imagine that I'm in the Alps, on my skis. But then Sebastian spoils my dream by zooming past me, waving and reminding me that I'm not that good at skiing anyway; just like everything else, I'm actually quite rubbish. But I don't care because I'm almost certainly never going to go skiing again. Now we're poor, I'm probably doomed never to do anything fun ever again.

I get bored of ceiling gazing and busy myself unpacking my trunk and arranging my belongings. I'm not sure if we're allowed to put pictures on the walls, so I leave my posters in my trunk and put it at the end of my bed like a little seat. I make the bed with my duvet and stuff from school, then try out the mauve plastic blinds. They don't work very well so I pull them back up quickly so no one can accuse me of breaking them and sit quietly on my bed, waiting for my new life to begin.

After about half an hour of waiting, nothing in my new life has happened. My dad hasn't come to find me and I haven't gone to find him. We're like hide-and-seek gone wrong. Everybody's hiding and no one is seeking. We're just sitting waiting for something to happen. My tummy's rumbling. I missed lunch at school and I was too scared to ask my dad to stop for food on the way. I can hear a quiz programme blaring out from the television, filling our quiet flat with other people's laughter and clapping and cheerful sounds. I should probably go and join him but I'm scared, I don't want to make him angry again. I pull out my book of 100 favourite poems, flick through it and wish Matron had given me a book on 100 top tips on what to do when the credit crunch has turned your life upside down. It would have been more useful right now than poems.

After another hour of waiting, I am so bored with looking at poems that even a maths lesson would seem like fun, so I decide to go and explore. I'm nervous and can't stop scratching the patch of worry eczema that's popped up on my wrist. I'm *really* hungry and my dad must be *starving*, as he looks like he hasn't eaten for days. I can't remember my dad ever cooking dinner for me. I can remember him flying through the door and bolting his food down before going off for a business meeting or a game of squash at the gym, but cooking isn't something he's able to do. All he's really good at is work.

Eventually I creep out of my room and explore the dingy kitchen. I find a tub of margarine, a tomato and a litre of milk in the fridge. In the cupboard on the wall are two tins of baked beans with sausages, half a loaf of bread and some instant coffee. I make us both some beans and sausages on toast and even though I don't actually like coffee, I make a mug for each of us to have with our meal. Maybe helping out will make him like me more.

"Eat your dinner, Daddy, " I say, "before it gets cold."

He doesn't reply. He's just staring at the telly, like I don't exist any more.

"I made us some food," I say, a little louder. "I thought you'd be hungry, Daddy."

He just keeps staring, so I balance his food on his lap and put a knife and fork in his hands. An old memory of how to eat food sparks up in his brain and he eats and eats and eats, without saying one word, until his plate is empty. I take it from his lap and give him his coffee, which he quickly drinks down.

"Do you need anything else, Daddy?" I ask.

"What do you think I need?" he storms, his words flashing through the room like lightening. "It's a pretty stupid question, Liberty, isn't it? But then I suppose that's why you don't seem to be able to get on very well at school. Even a fool could work out what I need. I need money! I need a job! I need a life! Look at me! I'm ruined! And if you think a plate of beans on toast is going to make it all better, you'd better think again."

I shrink back into myself, wishing I could disappear into the sofa, and then he'd never have to bother with me again. I keep my eyes on the carpet and my body very still. One wrong move and he'll get more furious. One wrong word and I'm dead.

I hate my dad. I wish I could get up and shout my own head off at him and say mean stuff like, "Failure is not an option for a Parfitt, blah, blah, blah." Or, "You're letting the side down, Henry Parfitt, time to pull your socks up and put your head down and find the money to send me back to school where I belong." But I don't because I'm frozen to the sofa like a statue, not daring to move.

Chapter 7
School..?

The next morning my dad is still sitting where I left him. The beardy stubble on his face has grown a little longer, his skin is a little greyer and his eyes look darker and more tired and far away. He's staring at breakfast telly like it's the most interesting thing he's ever seen in his whole life. I peep in at him and try to say hello but the words get stuck in my throat; I think they're too scared to come out in case he bites their heads off. I go and have a shower instead.

The shower in the bathroom doesn't work properly. It keeps going from freezing cold to boiling hot and I have to dance in and out of it and try to wash myself quickly when it lands on warm. This bathroom is rubbish. It's got black mould growing in the bits between the tiles and it's spreading like some deathly disease all over the walls. I shrink away from it, not wanting to catch anything bad. My bathroom in our London house was made from soft, cool marble and the decorator put things like lighthouses and starfish all about the place to give it a seaside feel. At least I have my old sand-coloured towels here to dry myself with. At least they're clean and uncontaminated.

I dry myself and wrap up in my bathrobe, which smells all friendly of school, then make us both some coffee and toast with sliced tomato. I'm getting used to the taste of coffee and decide that I actually even quite like its rich, roasty flavour, just like that advert says. My dad's used to our old housekeeper, Maureen, making his breakfast for him, so if I wasn't here to do it I truly think he'd starve. There's hardly anything left in the cupboards and I'm worried about what we'll have for supper. But I'm not going to ask him what's going to happen. I don't care if we die from starvation.

"Your uniform's in the plastic bag on my bed," my dad barks, making me jump, because I thought he'd actually forgotten how to speak. "You start school at 8.45. Turn left as you come out of the flats and keep going straight until you get there. It's simple. Then go to the office and they'll tell you where to go and what to do and how the whole free school lunch thing works. It's all sorted, OK?"

"School?" I whisper.

"Of course, school," he barks. "What did you think, Liberty, that you were going to laze around the place all day long watching daytime telly? Of course you've got to go to school, that's what children do, isn't it? And with your poor academic record, Liberty, you haven't got a moment to spare. Go and get stuck in! And I want you to make a good impression, do you hear? Don't let me down."

I wish I could ask if I can wait until Monday morning, because starting school on a Friday seems pointless to me. I wish I could ask if I can have some time getting used the idea of a new school and a new life, but I can't, so I swallow my words down with a bitter sip of coffee.

My dad's bedroom is a mess. There are a few huge old trunks that I don't recognise stacked in the corner, loads of plastic bin bags full of clothes and stuff, a suitcase and some dusty boxes that look like they've come from our London house attic. There's a pile of Sebastian's medals and trophies on the floor and masses of important-looking paperwork toppling off Dad's bedside table. His bed's not made up and I can see stains on the mattress left behind from people who've lived here before. There's a fresh pile of starched cotton sheets, cleaned and ironed by Maureen, our old housekeeper, waiting to go on. But they look all wrong here in this stupid old flat, they look all sad and shy and out of place.

I rummage through the piles of stuff until I come across a carrier bag of clothes that look like they might be my school uniform. Next to them I spy a battered old violin case that's completely covered in dust. I've never seen it before and I can't quite believe my eyes. I rub them to make sure I've not gone completely mad and started seeing things that aren't real. But when I look again it's still there, lying on the bed like the best treasure I have ever seen in my whole life. I'm dying to open it and pull the violin out and play. My skin is glittering all over with excitement and I can already feel the music washing right over me and carrying me away to paradise. But I can't open it, can I? My dad would go mad, especially if I started playing it first thing in the morning. He doesn't even know I can play. I'd make him splutter his coffee all over himself in shock. But what is a violin doing on his bed anyway? My dad hates music, everybody knows that. So how did it get here? Who does it even belong to?

Relief starts flooding through me. Maybe he's changed his mind? Maybe with the credit crunch and everything he's decided to stop fighting me about music? A frog jumps into my head with an idea in its mouth. It's my birthday next week; maybe he got the violin for me as a surprise? Maybe he got it to make up for me having to leave my school and everything else in my life behind? Maybe he isn't so mean after all? I actually can't believe it; my dad's finally got me a violin! I know everything will be OK when I'm allowed to play. It won't matter where we live or what stupid school I have to go to.

I decide not to say anything because I don't want to spoil his surprise. Instead, I draw a tiny heart in the dust, and then rub it out quickly so my dad won't see.

My new uniform is very different from my old one. It's more relaxed. I have a pair of black trousers, a red polo shirt and a black jumper with red stitching on it that reads "Cherry Grove Community School". And there's a blazer with a badge that has an embroidered picture of a red cherry tree and the Latin words: *Prosperitus est non quis vos perficio, est quisnam vos es* written underneath. I search in my brain to remember some Latin words from my old school and work out that my new school motto is saying something about success, so my dad will be pleased with that.

Chapter 8

The grave...

The stairway out of our flats is very busy at 8.25 in the morning. There are people in smart suits with briefcases and mums with buggies and babies and kids wearing the same clothes as me, all pushing and shoving their way down the stairs. I turn left like Dad said and follow the trail of black and red uniforms that spills out onto the street. I'm scared. I've heard all about state schools from other people at my old school and they sound noisy and rough and big. Alice's cousin says there are loads of fights and people get hurt. Maybe I should have argued harder with my dad and Mr Jenkins and forced them to let me stay.

What I don't understand is why my dad is always so mean to me and not to Sebastian? Sebastian gets everything he wants. I've been as good as gold my whole life and tried so hard not to make a nuisance of myself, but still my dad holds me as far away as possible from him, like I've got sick all down my front and am covered in a highly contagious rash. But none of that matters now. I can forgive him for it all because he's got me a surprise violin for my birthday. A warm little rush of excitement races through my body and makes me want to skip.

Down on the street an old man is struggling to get into his old people buggy car thing. He's puffing and panting and struggling to get his legs moving. When he sees me he calls out.

"You seen Cali this morning?" he asks.

"Sorry," I say, "I'm new here, I don't know who Cali is. Can I help?"

"I just need a hand," he says. "If I can just rest on your arm a minute then I can pull this stupid old leg up and get on. It's lottery day, you see, I've got to get my ticket. It's a £13 million rollover."

"Hi," says a girl with a million tiny plaits in her hair, tied with multicoloured braid. "You need a hand, Ivor?"

"There you are," says Ivor, looking relieved at Cali's arrival. "I thought you'd abandoned me for the day."

"You know I'd never do that, Ivor," she laughs, helping him into his buggy, like she's done it a hundred times before.

"Haven't seen you around before," says Cali, when Ivor is safely in his buggy and heading off towards the shops and we're making our way to school.

"We've just moved here," I say. "I'm Liberty Parfitt, what's your name?"

"I'm Cali," she says. "You know, you wanna tone down that accent of yours, it'll get you into trouble at The Grave. The other kids will eat you alive! But stick with me, Libs, and you'll be safe. What year you in?"

"Seven."

"Cool," she smiles, "same as me. Where did you find that accent, Libs? It's terrible! You sound like you're related to the Queen or something."

"Not sure," I say, trying hard to listen to my own voice. "I've always had it, I suppose."

Then Cali cracks up laughing and staggers around in fits of giggles. "Well, if you take my advice, girl, you'll ditch it pretty soon. Fitting in is what it's all about at

The Grave, and accents like yours just don't. OK?"

"OK. Why do you call it 'The Grave'?" I ask.

"You'll see," she says, "soon enough. You sure do have a lot to learn, Libs, but first off you gotta start dropping your T's and you gotta shake your voice up a bit. Speak easy, like me. Like cas-u-al."

"I'll try," I say, "but it's just natural to me, I don't know how I would even begin to change it."

"That's where I come in," she says. "Just listen real careful to me and you'll pick it up in no time. Pretend you're acting or something, you know? Oh, and The Grave? It's Cherry Grove, Cherry *Grave*, get it? It's like a graveyard inside those walls. Nothing good ever happens; it's just rubbish, Libs. All the teachers and most of the kids are like the living-dead, sucking graveyard air," Cali makes a spooky face, "and no one even cares about the education. It's more about surviving than learning. It's a dead-end place from beginning to end, preparing you for rubbish jobs when you leave. Except for me that is, Liberty Parfitt. Me? I've got *big* plans. *I'm* going somewhere. You'll see. So, why did you move here then?"

"Credit crunch," I say. "My dad's business went bust

so I had to leave my school. We're staying in a friend's flat until we get back on our feet."

"Posh school, I bet?" she asks. "I was born to go to one of them, I promise you! I'm bright enough. It's just the stork got lost on the way and I got delivered to the wrong family."

"It was just school to me," I say. "I'd been there since I was seven years old. But I'm not there any more, Cali, I'm here and I need to get on and get used to it, just like everything else in my life."

When we reach The Grave, thousands of kids swarm like black and red bees through the gates. Unfamiliar sounds buzz around me and I can't quite tell if I'm more scared or more curious. In all of Alice's wildest dreams and in all of mine, we couldn't have imagined that I'd find myself in a place like this. But here I am amidst a thousand black and red bees; with my new friend Cali, who has a million tiny plaits in her hair tied with multicoloured braid.

Cali comes to the school office with me and somehow manages to persuade the lady there to let me be in the same class as her. She promises to be my "class buddy" and show me around. The corridors here are long and grey and dark and smell of old cabbage and disinfectant. There are no flowers decorating the place, like in my old school and no gold carpets on the floors. Instead, everywhere is decorated with black and red bumblebee children zooming along the corridors and screeching up and down the stairs.

"Slow down, ladies and gentlemen," shouts a teacher, "and keep your voices down."

But no one listens. Everyone just carries on running and screaming. No one holds doors open for other people or offers to carry the teachers' heavy bags. I feel small in this big place and am worried that I won't fit in. I wish I hadn't tied my hair back so neatly, I look stupid. I pull off my hair tie and shake my hair loose.

"Cool hair," says Cali, looking at my bright red curls.

"Yours too," I smile.

At my old school I knew every single child and teacher by name and everyone there knew me. Here I know nobody, except Cali and I'm glad to have her next to me, she somehow makes me feel brave, like I could even face my dad with her around.

My first lesson is drama. Our teacher is at least 190 years old and she makes us read scenes from Shakespeare's

A Midsummer Night's Dream. I quite like Shakespeare, but all the rest of the kids are groaning with boredom. Shakespeare's only fun if you know how to read it properly, otherwise it's just a string of difficult words that are hard to understand. My old drama teacher taught us to read it in time with a heartbeat, that way the whole thing suddenly comes alive.

A boy with spiky hair, who is called Dylan, is interrupting our reading by having a fight with our teacher, Mrs MacDougall. He's going on about the fact that she's infringing his human rights by asking him to turn his mobile phone off during lesson time and Mrs MacDougall is trying to give him a calm and reasoned argument to dispute this. I know she's not really feeling calm inside because a little stream of sweat is running down her face and on to her blouse collar, making a stain. I am shocked. I have never seen a pupil argue with a teacher before.

A girl with white-blonde hair holds up a red card and runs out of the room.

"She's allowed to do it," says Cali, seeing my surprise. "She has an anger problem, which means she sometimes just bursts into one big rage that disrupts the whole class and frightens the teachers. So it's better for everyone if she gets herself to the 'green room' as quickly as possible to calm herself down."

Clusters of girls are whispering and giggling and not paying attention to any of what's going on. Some boys at the back of the class are shooting bits of squished up paper through their biros to see who can be first to hit the bull's-eye, which happens to be Mrs MacDougall's head. There's so much going on in our classroom that my eyes don't know where to look next and I'm finding it hard to keep my attention on Shakespeare. Cali is sighing and gently bashing her head on the table in despair.

"See what I mean?" she says. "It's terrible here, we never get anything done. It's so boring. Why can't they just get on with it and they might even discover that they actually like Shakespeare! I bet nothing like this ever happened at your old school. You wait, we'll just about be getting into it and we might even learn something and then the bell will go and we'll have to pack all our stuff up and go on to our next lesson."

Cali is right because before we know it, the bell's ringing and we're off to a P.E. lesson. We all get changed into black and red-striped P.E. kits and buzz around the sports hall trying to play basketball. But basically the whole lesson turns into one big fight and the teacher has to separate the culprits and abandon the game.

"You're right, Cali," I say, when we're in the changing room, "nothing like this ever *did* happen at my old school. But I don't know how you can call this place a graveyard. Madhouse, maybe, but graveyard, never!"

Chapter 9

Like Pride and Prejudice and stuff...

At lunchtime things get really bad. I stick close to Cali and she shows me how the canteen works. I make sure I get a big helping of Friday fish and chips and a double helping of sponge and custard for pudding. I don't know if there'll be anything but coffee and margarine for supper when I get home.

"Hi, Cali," says Dylan, coming to sit with us and unloading his lasagne from his tray. "Who's your new la-di-da friend then?"

"This is Liberty," smiles Cali. "Libs for short and give her chance Dyl, she's learning fast."

"Hello, Dylan," I say. "Pleased to meet you."

Then he cracks up laughing and sticks his nose up in the air and starts talking in a funny voice, "Oh, sorry, I'm so very pleased to meet you too, Liberty. Perhaps later I might take you for a lovely wander in the rose garden?"

Then he starts laughing again until tears squeeze out of his eyes and I don't think he can stop.

"You're like something out of one of them Jane Austen stories," he laughs, "like *Pride and Prejudice* and stuff. My mum loves them."

"I'm not really," I say, blushing and feeling awkward. "I just speak differently, I guess. It doesn't mean anything though. Not really. I can't help it."

"'It doesn't mean anything though,'" he mimics.

"Calm down, Dylan," says Cali, "she's not that funny. Why don't you turn your attention to helping her instead of laughing at her?"

So Dylan and Cali spend the rest of lunchtime attempting to teach me how to easy up my accent.

"I can't do it," I say, after trying really hard. My whole face starts glowing red with embarrassment. Their sounds feel weird in my mouth and however hard I try, my tongue keeps getting all twisted around them.

"You'll just have to try a little bit harder then, won't

you?" says a very big boy from the end of our table.

"Accents don't mean anything," I shriek, turning towards him. I can feel myself losing it again and I can't control myself. My rage is bubbling up inside, threatening to boil over. Alice's words about taking responsibility for my feelings are spinning around my head but I don't know what she means; I don't know how to take responsibility.

"Just because you think I have a posh accent," I scream, "it doesn't mean you know anything about me or about my life. You know nothing! Nothing! Nothing! Nobody does!" I throw my cutlery down so hard it breaks my plate in two. Cali puts her head in her hands.

"It means you're rich," the big boy shouts back. "Loaded, by the sounds of it. Listen to yourself. What you doing in a place like this anyway, poor little rich girl? Shouldn't you be out on your pony with Mummy? Rich girl, rich girl, poor little rich girl."

And then like a wave rippling through the dining hall the whole school joins in and chants, "Rich girl, rich girl, poor little rich girl."

Their loud words tumble over and over me and I'm drowning in a sea of noise. I hate them all. They know nothing about me or my life. If only they really knew what my life was really like and how much it's fallen to pieces in the past twenty-four hours, then they'd have nothing to shout about. But they haven't even given me a chance. I wish I could run away and disappear.

Cali starts sighing and banging her head on the table again.

"What is it with you?" she shouts above the noise. "You really let him get under your skin didn't you? You gotta learn to keep yourself under control here, Libs, otherwise you're gonna end up in deep, deep trouble. You gotta learn to stay cool, stay easy."

Everyone's still chanting and their noise is crashing over my head like rough, grey waves and there's nothing to hold onto. Then suddenly there's a huge uproar and the world's most massive food fight breaks out. Chips and sausages and lumps of fish and tomatoes and great blobs of lasagne are being flung from every corner of the room. Most of the kids are shrieking and shouting and going crazy. Everyone seems to have forgotten about me, they're too busy with their own food wars. Cali's eyes glitter at me and a daring smile tugs on her lips. My fingers dance around the edge of my plate, longing to join in. Nothing so outrageous as this ever happened at my old school and I'm caught in the middle of excitement and fear. Cali smiles and throws a chip at me and I can't resist it any more. I grab a handful and throw them back at her and then some fish and custard and pudding and we're all getting covered in food. Custard is sliming its way down my new blazer and Cali has fish batter stuck in her hair.

We're all laughing and screaming and then the big boy shoots an evil glare at me across the table. I quickly swallow my laugh and freeze and then stare right back at him. A blob of cold custard drips on to my cheek wiping the smile from my face. Alice wouldn't believe this if she were here; she wouldn't know what to do. She'd probably say, "Take responsibility, Libby." But I don't care about what Alice thinks any more and I don't care what the stupid big boy thinks of me. He's not going to get away with bullying me, I've had enough of that from my dad.

I pick up a big chunk of sticky sponge pudding and fling it through the air towards him. The only trouble is that Mrs Cobb, our head teacher, bursts into the room and gets in the way. The sticky sponge splats on her glasses and slides slowly down her face before it plops to the floor. Everyone is silent and my sponge-throwing arm is completely frozen in midair. Mrs Cobb grabs the back of my blazer and pulls me towards the door.

Inside her office, I suddenly don't feel so brave.

"Explain yourself, Liberty," she says, rubbing cake crumbs off her jumper with one hand and leafing her way through a file, which I suspect is all about me, with the other. "There's nothing in your notes here to suggest that you're a troublemaker. Now tell me what happened?"

"Well," I say, my voice wobbling, and wishing I were back, safe and well behaved, at my old school, "everyone was laughing about my accent and they were calling me 'rich girl' and I said that accents don't mean anything about who you are, because they don't, and anyway I'm not even rich any more, and then the whole dinner hall went crazy. I'm sorry Mrs Cobb, for causing any trouble."

"Yes, well," she says, "I might expect that kind of behaviour from some of the others in this school, Liberty, but not from you. I understand from your father that you're experiencing a rather dramatic change in circumstance. So in this instance, I suggest you go to the bathroom and clean yourself up and we'll put it down to that and forget about the whole thing. I will, of course, expect you to join in the dining hall clean-up detention after school and then I don't expect to see you back in this office for anything of this nature again. Do I make myself clear?"

Chapter 10

Err, sorry, daddy...

I'm drowning in a hot puddle of detention shame, which is melting me into a jelly of badness. I am now officially a bad person and although Mrs Cobb is putting all this down to my change of circumstances, I am not so sure. Maybe my dad is right; maybe I've been a bad person all along. I don't want to look at anyone, so I try to stick my eyes to the floor, but they keep disobeying me and following the very big boy who started all the shouting. I can see him over the other side of the hall, scraping lasagne off the wall and he can see me. His shiny black eyes meet mine and he mouths the words, "You're dead" at me. A cold shiver races down my spine. The whole school is here quietly scrubbing away at bits of dried-out food and it's all my fault. Some of the dinner ladies and the school security man are pacing up and down, watching out for trouble. My hands are trembling and my throat is dry. My dad will go completely mad if he ever finds out about this and then I really will be the disgrace of the Parfitt family.

"I thought I told you to stay cool," says Cali, finding me when our detention hour is up and we're all allowed to speak again.

"I tried, Cali," I say, "but sometimes my temper is just too hard to control. And it wasn't all my fault. Everyone suddenly went crazy. I'm sorry you got a detention as well."

"It's not the detention I'm worried about," she whispers, "it's you getting on the wrong side of Tyler. He's evil."

"What might he do?" I ask.

"You really don't wanna know about that," she says, "it'll give you nightmares. Come on, stay close."

My eyes are all over the road on our walk home, looking out for Tyler. I can't see him but every time we pass a shop doorway I stick myself to Cali in case he's lurking in the shadows, waiting to leap out and get me.

"My advice would be to lie low for the weekend," says Cali. "Let him blow off his steam on other people. I'm around so if you're bored come on up. Fourth floor, orange door, number 119. My mum's a childminder, so just follow the kid noise and you won't get lost."

I'm left alone, staring at our green front door. I've managed not to think about my dad and his problems all day long, but now I'm home I can't pretend they don't exist any more. I'm scared he's going to shout at me and if he finds out about the detention, I'll definitely be dead. I take a deep breath and knock on the door. *It's OK,* I say to myself, *I can cope with this. I can cope with anything.* I haven't thought about the violin all day and now the thought of it makes me feel stronger. Soon I'll have a violin and I'll be able to disappear inside my music and take myself far away from here. I can hear the telly blasting out from the sitting room, but my dad can't hear me. I knock again, a little more loudly and wait. Nothing. I hold the letterbox open with my fingers and shout.

"Dad, it's me."

"All right, all right," he finally grumps, charging down

the hall. "I can hear you, Liberty, I can hear you. Haven't you heard of such a thing as a doorknocker?" he booms when he opens the door.

I shrink back into myself and silently slide inside. Nothing has changed from when I left this morning. I don't think my dad's even made himself a coffee let alone anything to eat. He still hasn't had a shower, so he's starting to smell and he's still wearing the same clothes from yesterday when he picked me up from school. He slumps back on the sofa and stares at the telly. I hover in the doorway waiting for him to ask about my day. But he doesn't. He just keeps on staring and staring and I wish he would notice me like he does Sebastian. I wish we could do things together and have fun and wish that just once in my life he might like me and say he's proud of me. Just once would be enough, just so I could know for sure. It might help if I had something pleasing to say, something to cheer him up and cheer me up and bring a bit of sunshine into our flat. But I'm full of dirty, grey dishwater and he's turned into a slug.

I make us both a coffee and we sip in silence while a man on the news talks about the credit crunch and all the bank problems and all the companies going bust and closing down. There are shops all over the place closing down, even ones that have been going for years. The man on the news keeps saying how it's going to affect everyone and the worst is yet to come. My dad just keeps on sighing and sighing; it's like he's lost in a black hole and can't seem to find his way out. I don't find the news very interesting. I mean I know it's important and everything but I just want to ask about the violin. The words keep trying to escape from my mouth but I don't think now is really the right time. It's my birthday soon and I'll just have to wait until then. But I can't wait for my birthday. I want to know now.

"Daddy," I say, "you know on your bed…?"

"Quiet, Liberty," he snaps. "Can't you see I'm trying to listen to the news?"

Later, after we've eaten some chips from the chip shop and my dad is staring at more news, I creep back into his room to look for the violin. I just need to see it, to know that it's real. I can't wait. I just have to know.

In his room everything is exactly as I left it this morning. Except for one thing. The violin has disappeared! I rub my eyes to wake them up and search around under the piles of stuff and in the bin bags, but it's nowhere. I can't believe it! It was definitely there this morning, I wasn't imagining it and now it's disappeared. Oh, please, please, please make me find it… please let it be here. I'll be good for ever and ever and ever and I'll never lash out or get detention again I promise, promise, promise! I don't want to spoil my dad's birthday surprise but I need, need, need to see it, just to make sure it's true. I'm just sliding under the bed, in case it got pushed under by accident, when my dad bursts his way into the room.

"What are you doing in here, Liberty?" he booms. "Can't a man have a bit of privacy in his bedroom any more? This is an out-of-bounds room, Liberty, do you hear me?"

"Err, sorry, Daddy," I say, standing up and brushing the dust off my uniform. "I was just going to make your bed up for you so you can go to bed tonight," I lie. "You're looking tired. I was just trying to help."

"Oh," he huffs. "Good idea, Liberty. Well get going on it then. Don't dally."

Chapter 11

My whole insides are trembling...

I can't sleep. Every time I close my eyes all I can see is Tyler's mouth saying, "You're dead." I make sure my window is shut tight and am glad for the sounds of the telly drifting under my bedroom door. My whole insides are trembling and my worry eczema's got so bad I had to put loads of special cream on before I went to bed. I pull out my phone. I know it's late but I'd like to talk to Alice, even though she's annoying me at the moment, I think the sound of her voice will help.

"Libby, I'm so glad you called," she whispers. "I've been worried to death about you. What's happening? Are you OK?"

"I'm OK… ish, Alice. I had to go to this new school and it's kind of all right, but they started teasing me about my accent and then there was a food fight and I got a detention and a big boy is threatening to kill me."

"Detention! You had a detention, Libby?" she shrieks. "Your dad will go mad at you when he finds out. You are so funny! Thea Quaddy's moved into your bed, we're having such fun. Missing you though."

"I'm missing you too," I say and then my voice cracks and I start crying. "It's horrible here, Alice, my dad's being really weird and I'm so scared of Tyler."

"I can't believe you got a detention, Libby, it's amazing! Wait till I tell the others. Sorry, I've got to go," she whispers, "Matron's coming."

"OK," I say, "but I need you to promise me that you won't tell Sebastian. It's none of his business what's happening here. And I can't call you often, Alice, because I've nearly run out of phone credit and you know…"

I can't stop crying. It's three o'clock in the morning and I can hear snooker championships on the telly. I snuggle close to my teddy. His name is Mr Ted and he wears a blue stripy jacket and yellow woollen trousers. My mum gave him to me the day I was born. If she were still alive none of this would be happening, I'd be having a lovely life where only nice things happen. If she were still alive I bet she'd go right up to stupid Tyler and punch him on the nose and tell him to leave me alone. She'd be able to sort my dad out and tell him to be friendlier to me and she'd probably be full of brilliant ideas to help him to get a job. And I'd never ever be scared again and if I were she'd always hold me tight and tell me not to worry. Maybe I should disobey my dad and call my granny. I could ask to borrow Cali's phone, I'm sure she wouldn't mind, especially as it would be a real life emergency. Granny would know what to do, she's good at solving problems.

I hear my dad switch off the telly and our flat fills up with the silence of the night. He's moving around, mumbling to himself, opening and closing the kitchen cupboards and slamming the fridge door. Now he's in his bedroom. It sounds like he's moving some of the heavy boxes and trunks around. There are clicking sounds and bashing sounds, and then he drops something and swears. I'm wondering about the violin. He's quiet for ages, then I hear him shuffling towards my door.

My tears freeze; I hold my breath and shut my eyes

tight. Please don't come in! Please don't come in! He peeps his head around the door, then creeps in and sits on the end of my bed. I can't believe it, he's crying. He's sobbing and shaking. I open my eyes a teeny bit to look and his tearful face is like crumpled paper, wet from the rain. I've never seen my dad cry before and I don't like it; it feels weird and confusing. One minute he's barking at me like a fierce dog and the next he's crying like a little boy. I lie really still so he thinks I'm asleep because I don't know what to do. I'm not interested in talking to him because every time I do, he just bites my head off. And anyway, he's not really interested in talking to me. He only wants Sebastian and that's the truth. I think I should be feeling sorry for him or sad. But I don't because my heart has shrivelled up into a little ball and is hiding somewhere safe inside. I don't want him in here; I wish he would leave.

"I'm sorry, Lissy," he sighs. "I'm so, so sorry. It's all my fault, all of it."

I think my dad's gone mad. Who on earth is he talking to? I know for sure that I am not Lissy, but who on earth is? Why can't he be like a normal dad and go back to his own room and leave me alone to sleep? But he doesn't go. It's gross; he's curling up in a ball and falling asleep on the end of my bed. I wriggle my legs out of the way so I'm not touching any part of him. He stays there for hours, his snoring keeps me awake and his stale breath smell keeps puffing up my nose. In the early hours of the morning he wakes up and quietly creeps away. I stretch my legs into the warm patch that his body leaves behind.

Chapter 12

Don't forget the old folk...

Usually my weekends are full of fun stuff like horse riding, violin playing and boarding house pizza and movie nights. This weekend is different. Since my dad's weird crying episode last night, all the air and anger has been let out of him and he's just moping about the place looking like a sad and soggy balloon. He keeps on staring at me with these big watery eyes, like he thinks I know what we should do to get us out of this mess. And every now and then he just bursts into uncontrollable tears.

When we pop to the supermarket, I'm on red alert for Tyler and I put my head down as we pass the gangs of boys lurking in the street. Living on benefits means we have to be careful about what we buy. I take charge and lead my dad down the vegetable aisle. Healthy eating is important, even if we don't have any money. My dad's used to having millions of pounds in the bank to spend on anything he likes, so he keeps picking up all the expensive stuff. Our fridge in our old house was huge. We had an icemaker and double-opening doors and it was crammed full to the brim with every type of food you could imagine. Our fridge in our flat now is tiny. It sits under the worktop and has little bits of old food mouldering away in the rubber seal around the edge of the door. I have to keep pulling Dad's expensive shopping out of the basket without him noticing and exchanging it for stuff we can afford. The affordable stuff looks boring. The packaging is plain and dull and I bet it tastes disgusting. Alice would do a pretend vomit at the thought of eating cheap food. But I don't have any choice now, do I? It's all right for her she doesn't have to get used to life in the credit-crunch zone. She's floating above it all in la-la land.

I take Cali's advice and lie low for the weekend. I make myself some snacks and settle down with my iPod. My dad's lying on the sofa watching telly and eating biscuits, so he won't even notice. I close my door, lie under my duvet and plug myself in. The music immediately takes me to a far, far away place. I feel as if I'm on a white sandy beach, like the one near our French house, with gentle lapping waves and sand trickling through my fingertips. I can almost feel the cool water glittering in and out of my toes and swishing back across the sand. And now I'm in California and three dolphins are leaping and twirling and calling to me to play. The music has turned my body into a helium balloon and I'm floating high above the world, a million miles from here. And if I hold my hand out far enough I can almost touch the cool, white moon and fly through infinity into the glittering night sky. Nothing can hurt me here. Nothing! Not even Tyler, not even my dad's snappy words.

I spend most of the weekend plugged in to my iPod and my dad spends most of it plugged into the telly. We've built a castle of sound around us that is keeping our worries away. Neither of us talks much because there's really nothing to say and I'm worried that if I do talk I'll set my dad off on another fit of crying. I'm not sure what's worse, his shouting or his tears. Both of them grip their claws into my tummy and pinch me tight, leaving me feeling sore. By Sunday afternoon I'm so bored I go on up to Cali's.

Cali's whole flat is bursting with life and smiles and noise. Little kids are all over the place playing with toys, making things from card and glitter and glue and crowding around Cali's mum looking for cuddles.

"Hi," she calls to me, "you must be Liberty. Cali told me all about you. My name's Hanna. Come on in and make yourself at home."

Hanna clears a space for me on the crowded sofa and tells me to sit down. I've never been in a house like this in my life. For a start, our flats are small and you'd never imagine that you could fit so many people into one small space. And for another thing, the place is full to the brim with colourful stuff and toys and kids' paintings on the walls and clothes tumbling out of a wash basket and rainbow rugs and multicoloured scatter cushions. It's homely and warm and I like it because I feel welcome. Most of the houses I've visited in my life feel like they've been cut out of a page in a glossy magazine and they make me want to hold myself all neat and quiet and still.

Cali cuts us some slices of warm, freshly baked honey cake and we escape from the kids' noise and into her room. Her room is amazing. The walls are painted deep red and they're covered in posters from all the Broadway musicals. She's got *Cats* and *Les Misérables* and *Phantom of the Opera* and at least a million more. And she has this amazing mirror with lights all around it like something from a Hollywood film.

"Have you seen all of these shows, Cali?"

"Nah," she says. "We've never got enough spare cash to go to stuff like that. But one day, Libs, I'm going to *be* in one. I promise you. I'll have the star part and I'll post you tickets for my opening night and we'll ride in a limousine and drink champagne."

I've been in a limousine a hundred times before, but I don't tell Cali because I don't want to hurt her feelings.

"Don't forget the old folk, Cali," says Hanna peeping her head around the door.

"As if I would," smiles Cali.

"Good girl. Why don't you take Liberty with you?"

So Hanna loads us up with honey cake and flasks of homemade hot soup and Cali and I have to take it round to all the old people in our flats.

"My mum's obsessed with helping people," explains Cali. "She's set up this Community Action Scheme so that vulnerable people can get the help they need."

First we go into Len's flat. Len is ninety-five years old. I've never seen anyone so old before and he has wiry grey hairs growing out of his nose and ears.

"Tell your mum she's an angel," he says while he's slurping on his soup. "She'll have many a feather on her wings when she gets to heaven. And you too by the looks of things."

Cali sets me on to washing up while she vacuums Len's flat. Then we empty his bins and carry his rubbish down to the bin bay in the car park.

"Do you do this every weekend?" I ask Cali.

"Most," she smiles. "I don't mind, really. I mean, I'll be old too one day and there are benefits, you'll see."

After we've been to eighty-nine-year-old Ivor's flat and to seventy-eight-year-old Jean's, we climb to the top of the building to see eighty-year-old Joyce.

"I always save the best till last," smiles Cali, knocking on a bright pink door. "She always give me food and never makes me work."

"Daaaarrrrrlings," says Joyce, wrapping us in her arms

and planting pink lipstick kisses on our cheeks. "Come on in, come on in."

Joyce's flat is amazing. Everything is pink and I mean *everything*, even the piano sitting in the corner of the room. And the best thing is that she doesn't need any house cleaning or chores done, all she wants is company. Cali and I make us all a pot of tea. We get out Joyce's best pink tea set and slice the honey cake into three. When we're all stuffed full, our afternoon really begins.

"Read the newspaper to me will you, girls?" asks Joyce. "You two can take turns reading out loud."

Cali and I take turns reading out bits from the paper. It's so full of credit-crunch stories that I can't believe my eyes and ears. Businesses and banks and shops all over the place are closing down, even shops that have been open for years and years and years. Loads of people are losing their money and ending up in situations like my dad and me. I wonder about where they're all living now. Maybe some of them are in flats like me with mums and dads who can't stop crying and shouting.

"Stop now," says Joyce after a while. "This is all too depressing for me. I don't know, what is the world coming to? Time for a song, I think; something to cheer us all up. Do you like singing, Liberty?"

I nod and Cali's eyes shine and we're up and at the piano in a flash. Joyce totters over, plops herself down at the stool and pulls out a big fat music book full of 100 Best Musical Songs. We work our way through all of Cali's favourites and she's so excited by it all, but I can't really concentrate. The credit-crunch stories are travelling round my brain in a bus full of worry.

Chapter 13

The rest is a blur...

On Monday morning gossip is buzzing round the school. Mrs MacDougall's husband has had a heart attack and needs nursing, so she's left school until further notice and a new drama teacher is arriving this afternoon.

"I can't wait to tell Joyce," screams Cali, jumping up and down like a five-year-old. "I just hope whoever comes is a better teacher than Mrs MacDougall. I'm telling you, Hollywood here I come! What d'you wanna to be when you grow up, Libs?"

"It doesn't matter," I sigh, "it's too late now anyway."

"What's too late?"

"It's too late to be a proper violinist and that's all I've

ever wanted to be. You have to start playing when you're really young to truly be successful at it and I've only had second-hand lessons from my friend, Alice. I'll never make it now, so just forget about it, OK."

"Never say never," she smiles. "That's my mum's favourite motto."

At lunchtime I keep my head down and my mouth closed. Cali and Dylan stay close to me and we somehow manage to stay out of Tyler's way. Our last lesson is drama and when we all pile into the drama studio it's clear that things in Cherry Grove Community School are changing before our very eyes. The stage lights are on, the piano lid is open and a man wearing a red satin waistcoat and a yellow bow tie is beckoning us to hurry on in.

"Welcome, welcome, welcome, ladies and gentlemen," says the man, running his fingers up and down the piano keys. "Welcome to Broadway! I'm Mr Forrest, your new drama teacher, so come, come," he smiles, "gather round and let us begin."

Mr Forrest is brilliant! We spend the entire lesson learning songs and dances for our school Christmas production of *Bugsy Malone*. Cali is over the moon of course and is bursting with tales of our brilliant time singing and dancing with Joyce.

"You'll have to make sure she has a ticket to come to our production," Mr Forrest smiles.

The auditions are on Friday and we have to sing a song and read a piece from the script. Cali wants to play the part of Blousey Brown and Dylan's going for Bugsy. He's already trying to act all cool, like a 1930s American gangster and he hasn't even got the part yet.

"I can't believe we're doing a real live musical performance," Cali squeals, when we're heading out of the playground, on our way home. "It's gonna be such fun and I'll have a new poster to add to my collection, with my name on the front! Which part are you gonna audition for Libs?"

"In a perfect world I'd love to be part of the orchestra," I say, "to play the violin. But that's never going to happen, except if my dad… that is… on my birthday… Oh, I don't know, Cali, it's all a bit complicated."

"I've told you once already, Libs," says Cali, "never say never, OK? You have to keep following your heart and refuse to give up, just like me."

"It's all right for you, Cali," I snap. "Your mum's cool,

you can do what you want, but it's not like that for me. And in any case, I don't even have a violin."

My rage starts bubbling up, hot and fiery inside me. I'm angry at Cali, I'm angry with my dad and I'm angry at the world. I hate everyone and I hate my life. I wish I were dead like my mum. I storm off ahead and ignore Cali when she shouts for me to stop. Why should I listen to her? She doesn't own me, she can't tell me what to do. The red fire burns in my eyes and ears and closes in around me like a fog. I don't see Tyler coming towards me. The rest is a blur.

"I hate little rich girls," he screams in my face, trying to intimidate me, "and I especially hate them when they get me a detention. I lost my after-school job last night because of you, rich girl, so you owe me. Do you hear?"

But I don't hear him. I don't hear anything because of the red rage in front of my eyes. The fire burns up through my body filling my fists with power. I'm sick of people shouting at me and I'm sick of everyone telling me what to do all the time. I've had enough of it and it's going to stop, right now! I've spent my life being a yes girl, always trying to please everyone and it hasn't got me anywhere. The heat inside me is so hot that it turns into steam and Tyler doesn't know what's hit him. He's the kind of boy that *everyone* in a school is scared of; he's the kind of boy that no one stands up to; he's the kind of boy who rules the playground with an atmosphere of fear. But not any more! I'm not afraid of anyone! I dump my bag and start lashing out. It's not like usual, where I just shout and throw things, this is more serious, because *I'm* more serious now and this time I mean trouble, BIG TROUBLE!

I lunge towards him and throw an unexpected punch at his nose. I catch him unawares and his eyes flash with pain.

"Come on then, rich girl," he taunts, "show me what you've got."

I throw another punch, which misses and makes Tyler laugh. His laugh is like petrol on my flames and I throw myself into him scratching, spitting and tearing at his blazer, kicking his shins. Screams that sound like they belong to someone else are raging from my throat and ringing in my ears. When I catch Tyler's eye, things go from bad to worse, because they're twinkling with amusement and a great grin is spreading across his face.

He's managed to grab my wrists and is holding me at arm's length and laughing out loud.

"Show me what you've got, rich girl," he laughs.

"I've had enough," I shout, "do you hear me, Tyler? I've had enough!"

But he just keeps on laughing and laughing in my face and he's so big and strong compared to me that I'm flailing about like a mouse being held down by its tail. His amusement turns me into a great white shark and I start biting his hands and pushing at him and kicking and kicking at his shins.

"Ouch… Eeh… Ohh…" he puffs, trying to get his hands away from my mouth. "You're a right little number, you are. Go girl, go on, give me some more, I can take it."

And he just keeps laughing and laughing. He's not fighting back and he's not hurting me in any way. He's just holding me away, trying to protect himself from my claws. My rage keeps flowing, coming from deeper and deeper inside me and the more he laughs the more I fight.

A crowd has gathered around us and kids are chanting, 'Fight! Fight! Fight!'

90

Just before Mrs Cobb grabs the back of my blazer, Tyler whispers into my ear, "You're all right, you are, Liberty Parfitt. Respect!"

"I didn't expect to see you back here so soon, Liberty Parfitt," says Mrs Cobb when we're standing in her office. "I made an allowance for yesterday's behaviour, but today, I feel you have gone just one step too far. I have zero tolerance for violence in my school. Do I make myself clear?"

I just stare at the floor, not knowing what to say. My legs have gone all weak and I'm worried I might faint.

"Please explain yourself," she says, flashing an icy smile.

Tyler is glaring at me. He's trying to tell me something with his eyes and although I can't work out what he means, I do know that I really will be dead if I get him into any more trouble.

"It was all my fault, Mrs Cobb," I say. "Tyler did nothing, I felt angry and I just took it out on him. I'm sorry, it won't happen again, I promise."

Tyler's shoulders relax. He looks relieved.

"Double respect," he winks, when Mrs Cobb finally

frees us from her jaws, "except you still owe me, remember. You lost me my job at the tyre place and somehow you have to pay. After that I'll leave you alone. A debt's a debt, Liberty Parfitt and if you're gonna start playing with big boys then you have to play by big boy rules. Your Barbie days are over."

Chapter 14

If you're going to run wild...

My hand trembles like jelly when I knock at our front door because I know that Mrs Cobb will have phoned my dad by now and told him all about my fight with Tyler. I'm so stupid! I can't believe myself! I've never had a fight with anyone before and now I've gone and ruined everything and made things worse and got myself a bad reputation with my new head teacher before I've even had a chance to settle at The Grave. My granny will be furious if she finds out, even if it means agreeing with my dad for once. And my granny, when she's furious, is not a pretty sight. I don't know what's happened to me. It's as if some alien monster or something has abducted me and decided to ruin my life. I don't even understand what happened. I just kind of evaporated and got lost inside my rage.

When my dad lets me in we don't look at each other. Disappointment and tears are sitting heavy in his eyes, but there's no steam left inside him to even begin to talk about my fight. He trudges back to our sitting room, slumps down on the sofa and carries on staring at the telly. I'd prefer it if he'd get cross with me and send me to my room and ground me, or something like that. His silence hurts more. I change out of my uniform and make us both a coffee. I wish I could change things and make my life all better and back to normal. I wish I could get my dad's business back and all our money too. I wish I could get Tyler his job back and sort everything out. I've ruined things for everyone. The food fight wasn't Tyler's fault; it was mine for not being quicker at changing my accent. I should have listened harder. Now I can see why Cali was so keen for me to learn. I'm so useless.

Finally, my dad shuffles in to see me. He slumps down on my bed like a sack of old potatoes and then his eyes well up again and he starts blubbing.

"I've nothing left to say to you," he sobs. "I feel

humiliated, Liberty, shocked and humiliated by your behaviour, but I'm too exhausted to do anything about it. Can't you see I have enough of my own problems to be dealing with, without you adding to them? I wash my hands of you – if you're going to run wild then you'll have to face the consequences, alone."

I stare at the carpet and twiddle my fingers round and round. I don't know what to say but I know that I'm expected to say something.

"Sorry," I whisper and again it's like the word has caught the edge of a flame and whooshed up in my face.

"Sorry doesn't mean anything," he storms. His face puffs up all red like someone's pumped angry air back into him. Although I know he's going to go on and on for ages, something deep inside me relaxes. His anger is easier to be with than his tears. "You keep on saying sorry," he rages, "but nothing seems to change. You keep on messing up, Liberty, and I don't know what to do with you. And violence! At this rate you're going to end up in serious trouble. It's a tough world out there. I might have thought that for once you'd think about someone else other than yourself…"

I switch my ears off and imagine my dad shrinking. The

95

smaller he gets, the further away from me he is. Now he's just a tiny speck on the skirting board with a very big mouth that keeps opening and closing. I keep my face looking normal so he thinks I'm still with him, but actually I'm far away in a magnificent concert hall with a violin in my hand, ready to play. The orchestra is behind me, the conductor is in front of me and the audience is holding its breath, willing me to begin.

Eventually, my dad gets up and leaves the room. I switch my ears back on and close my door. I'm tired, so tired of everything and I wish somebody gentle would pick me up and carry me away. I find Mr Ted, give him a hug and then tell him all my troubles and amazingly he comes up with a very good idea.

All night long I'm tossing and turning. The seed of Mr Ted's idea starts growing into a very fine plan. I can't wait for the morning and the chance to at least put something right. When it gets light I'm up and ready and leave the house quietly without waking my dad. I race down the stairs and towards the town. There can't be that many tyre places round here and I have just about enough time to find the right one and still be in time for school. The first one I find is A.P. and Sons, Tyres and Exhausts. I'm a bit scared but I have to do this. Like my dad says, I have to start thinking of other people and not just myself. I make my way towards the office, where a big hairy man looks up from his desk.

"Does a boy called Tyler work for you?" I ask.

"Not here, love," the hairy man says. "You might try Tyre Right round the back of the market, that's the only other place that's local."

I'm running out of time, so I jog towards the market and down the little street behind. There are loads of cars queuing to get new tyres this morning because of the big sign at the end of the road saying "25 per cent Discount Day".

"Does a boy called Tyler work for you?" I ask a skinny boy who's using a loud machine to whizz the tyres off fast.

"He did," shouts the boy, over the machine, "but not any more. Why, who wants to know?"

"I do," I say. And then the whole story spills out and the skinny boy takes me to his boss who sits me down, makes me a coffee and perches on his desk to listen to me.

"I need you to give him his job back," I say. "I mean,

it's not fair, is it? It wasn't his fault he got the detention, it was mine."

When I start looking for Tyler at lunchtime, Cali can't believe her eyes.

"You're crazy," she warns. "Stay away from him, Libs, he's bad news."

"His bark is louder than his bite," I say and then I realise that the same is true for my dad. He might shout and rage and go on and on at me, but he's never actually hurt me. Well, not physically, that is. He has hurt my feelings though and I wonder which is worse.

"You really are all right, you are," smiles Tyler, when I tell him he's got his job back. "You've got spark, you have, I'm sorry I put you in the wrong box, Liberty Parfitt."

"Never judge a book by its cover," I brave.

Tyler gives me a high five and laughs, "Don't push your luck, pipsqueak."

Chapter 15

Today is my birthday...

Today is my birthday. I don't even know if my dad's actually remembered and I'm delaying getting up in case he hasn't, because I wouldn't know what to do or say and I don't know if I could actually just go off to school without mentioning it. If my mum were still alive I know she'd never forget my birthday. I think having a baby must be something a mum can never forget, even if they're far away and don't even see you. I'd like to think that my mum is remembering me today, even though she's dead. Maybe she'll be having a little tea party in the sky to celebrate me being twelve.

Twelve is big. It means I've got used to being double

figures and I'm only six years away from being eighteen, which must be amazing! A little flutter of hope is still alive in my heart. It keeps on reminding me that I did see a violin on my dad's bed and that the only person living in this flat that likes the violin is me. But there's also a big, fat heavy hammer in my head that keeps smashing my hope away. If my dad *had* planned a surprise for me I know that my recent behaviour would have definitely made him change his mind.

I haven't been with my dad on my birthday since I was six years old. My birthday is always in term-time, so usually I have them at school. My day always starts with Alice leaping on my bed, showering me with presents and glittery cards. Then we always do something special in our boarding house to celebrate, like having a movie and pizza and I *always* have a wonderful lemon cake with tea. My dad usually sends my present through the post and Sebastian always makes sure we eat lunch together or something like that. I wonder if Alice has remembered my birthday or whether she's so busy now with Thea Quaddy that she's totally forgotten I exist?

I stay in bed for as long as possible, without making myself late for school. I feel cosy and safe in here with

Mr Ted. When I'm up and dressed I creep out of my room and find my dad sitting at the kitchen table, waiting for me. He's made coffee and toast.

"Happy birthday, Liberty," he says, stretching a forced smile on his face. "I'm sorry it's not going to be a very exciting one, but here, I have this for you."

On the table is a long, fat box wrapped in pink paper and a pile of birthday cards. It's the kind of box that would most likely be able to fit a violin inside. Maybe my dad decided to disguise it so it would be a complete surprise. My heart is thumping fast.

"Go on then," he says, handing me a coffee, "open it."

"I'll start with my cards," I say.

My hands tremble as I open my cards. There's one from my granny in Scotland with five £20 notes in it and a message for me to buy myself something special and something sensible and to put some in the bank to save for a rainy day. She says she can't come to visit because she's off on an autumn cruise to the Caribbean, but she hopes I have a nice day.

"She wouldn't have been welcome anyway, silly old battleaxe," says my dad.

There's another card from our old housekeeper, Maureen, with a funny joke on the front saying, "What happened when the cat ate a ball of wool? It had mittens!" Ha, ha, not funny! And one from Sebastian, with a cool picture of a puppy wearing a tiara, sitting in a flowerpot. The one from my dad says, "To my Special Daughter" on the front. Tears prickle in the back of my eyes, because I know it's not true. The words should really say: "To my Especially Difficult and a Big Disappointment to the Parfitt Family Daughter", but I guess they don't sell cards that say those words.

"Go on," my dad urges in a gentle voice that he rarely uses on me, "open it up or you'll be late for school."

I can't open it. I'd like to ask if I could wait till later, but even then I know it'll be hard. I take a gulp of coffee and pick at the pink wrapping.

"It's a family heirloom," says my dad. "You know I haven't got any money for presents this year, but I thought you'd appreciate this; something special, to keep."

My heart leaps. Maybe it is true; maybe it is the violin. I pull the rest of the wrapping off, open the flaps of the box and peer inside. My dad's smiling, waiting for my reaction. My heart takes a big dive and lands with a thud in my stomach. I fix a fake smile on my face.

"They're wonderful, Dad," I lie, pulling the entire, leather-bound, *Complete Works of Charles Dickens* from the box. They're all there, *The Christmas Carol*, *Little Dorrit*, *David Copperfield*, *Oliver Twist*, all of them.

"They belonged to your Great-Grandmother Parfitt. You resemble her somewhat, so I felt they should be yours. She was a real bookworm, like you. I hope you enjoy them."

It's not until lunchtime that I can bring myself to tell Cali and Dylan it's my birthday. I've felt like bursting into tears all morning; even my own dad doesn't know that *I'm* not the bookworm, Alice is. If only I hadn't got into trouble I might actually have a violin of my own by now and I might have it here with me at school and I might be rushing to the *Bugsy* audition asking to play. But I can't exactly blame anyone but myself, can I? It's all my own stupid fault. I feel so sad and sorry about everything. I even feel sorry for my dad and *he* must feel terrible about not having enough money to buy me a proper birthday present.

The auditions for *Bugsy Malone* are about to happen. Joyce helped Cali prepare her song for her audition piece and she's so excited that she can't think or talk about anything else. Even Dylan is prepared. He's been learning lines and practicing an American gangster accent for days now which is actually getting really irritating, but it's good to see that at least some people are happy in this world.

"Aren't you going to audition for anything, Libs?" asks Dylan. "You should go for Lena, you'd be brilliant at her."

"No," I sigh. "I was hoping to be in the orchestra, but there's no hope of that now. I might do backstage or chorus or something, don't worry about me."

"Why is there no hope?" Cali pipes up. "You're so depressing sometimes, Libs. I mean, I know things aren't going so well for you at the moment, but you're not the only one, you know. Just take a look around this school; there are plenty of people suffering. None of us have the things we want, let alone the things we need. And I won't tell you again, remember, never say never, OK?"

"I'm sorry," I say, "it's just today is really bad. It's my birthday and I went and got this stupid idea in my head that my dad was going to get me a violin. But he didn't, he gave a set of stupid old books instead."

"Your birthday!" screeches Cali. "Why didn't you say?" And then her and Dylan break out into a *Bugsy Malone* style version of 'Happy Birthday' which makes me want to laugh and cry at the same time.

Chapter 16

I'm so sorry Liberty...

While Cali and Dylan are auditioning for *Bugsy Malone*, I come up with a brilliant plan. Cali's words are dancing in my head and she's right, I'm not the only one with troubles around here and it's about time I stop whinging and start taking some action. Just like Hanna with her Community Action Scheme. I follow the corridor away from the drama department. I don't know why it hasn't occurred to me before but obviously the best place to find a violin to play in *Bugsy Malone* is in the school music centre.

The music centre is quiet and dark. A few keyboards line the wall and a dusty old piano sits quietly in the corner. Mmmm... maybe this wasn't such a great plan after all.

"Can I help?" asks a lady with blonde hair, who I assume is one of the music teachers.

"Well," I whisper, "I was wondering about *Bugsy Malone* and if you had an orchestra playing for it?"

She laughs. "An orchestra! At *this* school? I wish! You must be new around here. My name's Mrs O, pleased to meet you." She holds out her hand. I shake it and introduce myself. "Luckily, a local professional orchestra has offered to play for us. Why, were you interested?"

"Yes," I say. "I'd like to play the little violin part at the beginning, you know, like on the film version, when they're eating in the Italian restaurant, just before the splurge attack? It's only a small part, I know, but I'd love to have it."

"Well," she says, "you're welcome to it. We were planning on having recorded music for that bit, but in fact it would be wonderful to have a real live player, what a lovely idea. Have you got a violin? How long have you been learning?"

Then I feel completely stupid standing here asking to play, because I have to answer no to both of her questions.

"Well," I say, blushing, "I can play a bit, but I'd need some lessons to learn the piece properly. And I don't have a violin, so I'd need to borrow something to play it on."

"I'm so sorry, Liberty," she says, "but I can't help. We're so short of funding in this place that we don't have any instruments for people to use, except those old keyboards. And to be honest most of the kids here aren't interested in orchestral kind of music anyway. But look," she says, picking up the *Bugsy Malone* music score and leading me to the photocopier, "take a copy of the music and I promise you, if you can get hold of an instrument and learn the piece, then the part is yours. OK?"

Well, at least I tried, and even Cali will have to admit that there's now, officially, no hope. I will never get to be able to play in *Bugsy Malone*. I'll just get involved in some backstage stuff. It will be better anyway. There'll be less chance of my dad finding out.

"Woooooo hooooooo!" squeals Cali after school, punching the air with her fist.

She's completely over the moon and back again because, of course, she got the part of Blousey Brown and she's dancing down the road singing 'I'm Feeling Fine' at the top of her voice.

"You see," she shrieks, "Blousey wants to get to Hollywood, just like me and we're both gonna get there, I promise you, I just know it! I'm made for the part, I was born to go to Hollywood."

Dylan isn't feeling so fine and neither am I. He didn't get the part of Bugsy, but he did get the part of Bugsy's right-hand man, Knuckles, so he's busy practicing cracking his knuckles like a gangster and pretending not to care. I try to act pleased for Cali because I know how much this means to her, so I join hands with her and make us spin around and around and around and I try to smile, but really I wish I could spin right away and disappear.

Today doesn't feel like my birthday. I haven't got that ice cream and birthday cake kind of feeling following me around and I think that with all the excitement of Bugsy, Cali and Dylan have actually forgotten as well. I wonder if Alice will remember and call me later? I hope she does.

"Bye, Libs," calls Cali, when we get to our flats.

I don't know why I feel so upset. I mean it's only a birthday, isn't it? It's no big deal. Who cares if I'm twelve now and not eleven? I mean, it doesn't show on my face, does it? And I'm not actually any different today, I mean it's not like it's a big birthday or anything, just a normal boring birthday and I need to start understanding that there are more important things going on in the world than my birthday.

My dad's staring at the telly again when I get home. I don't think he does anything else these days. There's certainly no evidence that he's out there searching for a job or getting busy with those pies he said he had his fingers in. I take my *Complete Works of Charles Dickens* into the sitting room and slump down on the sofa to have a good look through them. I superglue a convincing smile on my face; so good that no one would ever be able to read the disappointment that has written itself across my lips and hidden a sore little scar in my heart. So good that no one would ever guess that I'm even bothered one bit that the old books in my hands are not a violin and that I'll never get to play in *Bugsy Malone*. I wish I were brave enough to tell my dad how I feel. It must be lovely to be able to talk to your dad about things like that.

My dad keeps on looking at me out of the corner of his eye and I keep looking back at him, like we're both waiting for something birthdayish to magically happen. It must be hard for my dad; in our old life he'd just be able to dig his hand in his pocket and make anything happen. Money could fill the gaps, but now we can't do that sort of thing and we're left just sitting here with each other feeling awkward. Even when I was tiny my dad never properly did my birthdays himself. He would just hand out the cash to a nanny or a housekeeper who would try to make things nice. Or otherwise my granny would fly down from Scotland and interfere.

I try to get interested in the telly programmes, but my dad's obsessed with watching boring history stuff and quiz shows and the news. I don't like any of those so I make us both a coffee. I'm sure kids my age shouldn't be drinking so much of the stuff, but today I really, really just don't care. I guess, just to be polite I need to make a proper, enthusiastic start on Charles Dickens and begin at the beginning of one book and stay with it right the way through to the end. Alice would find this easy; she would eat all of them up in one day. And even Cali would probably be having them for tea right now, making them fun by acting out the old-fashioned characters, getting ready for Hollywood. But I can't seem to settle down to it. I keep checking my phone in case Alice has sent a text, but she hasn't and I feel nervous about calling her. I bet her and Thea Quaddy are best friends now and I'm just a distant memory. I'm not part of the rich-girl club any more; I can't do the things they do. Tempting birthday memories of Alice laughing and huge fat lemon cakes and thousands of presents keep dancing in front of my eyes.

Since the fight with Tyler, my angry feelings have melted into puddle of heavy sludge. I haven't got the energy for anger any more; I just don't care. My whole complete self has turned into one big fat, cold, grey day.

At six o'clock someone knocks at the door. My dad and I both jump out of our skins. We don't have visitors here; hardly anyone even knows where we live. My dad trudges up the hall to answer and I hover in the background curious to see who it is.

"Hi," says Hanna, all smiles. "I understand it's Liberty's birthday and if you don't have any plans I'd like to invite you both up for dinner."

Warm sunshine spreads through my body. Thank you! Thank you! Thank you God or Buddha or Allah or my mum or whoever might be watching over me. Thank you Cali and thank you Hanna. Thank you the world and the universe. I am here. I do matter. I smile back at Hanna and nod.

"Yes, please."

My dad's all of a fluster, he's running his hands through his bed-head hair and rearranging his clothes in an attempt to look smart in his jogging pants and smelly old shirt.

"Well," he stutters, "I'm not sure, really… Liberty and I… we…"

"Whatever," Hanna laughs. "See you both in fifteen minutes."

Chapter 17

For my new best friend...

Hanna is amazing. I wish she were my mum. She's filled her sitting room with streamers and balloons and pulled a table into the middle of the room and laid it with special birthday napkins and party poppers. And she didn't even know it was my birthday until Cali got home from school!

"Thank you so much," I whisper to Cali. "I was about to fall into a pit of despair, being left down there with my dad on my own all evening. I mean it's OK usually, there's nothing wrong with it, but... you know... it is my birthday."

"Cool," smiles Cali. "I'm glad you're happy. I love giving people surprises, it's fun."

"I thought you'd forgotten," I say, "what with *Bugsy Malone* and everything."

"Duh," she says. "When will you get it into your dumb head that I'm your friend, Libs? And friends don't forget each others' birthdays, not ever."

My birthday dinner is delicious. Hanna's made a spicy chicken thing with rice and sweet potato. My dad's lapping it up and *almost* smiling, but not quite. He actually looks quite awkward, like he's not sure what to do with his arms and legs. My dad's more used to smart restaurant dinners with limousines and champagne than cosy sitting room celebrations with apple juice. He changed into a fresh shirt and trousers before we came up and even managed to brush his hair and shave off his stubble. It's the first time in ages there's been a waft of his aftershave in the air. Apart from having lost some weight in the past few weeks, he almost looks like my dad again.

"I really appreciate this, Hanna," he says, "thank you. Things have been a bit difficult lately and you know…"

"You're very welcome," smiles Hanna, spooning more chicken on to his plate. "Think nothing of it, there's no need to explain."

When we've finished our main course there's a knock at the door.

"Party time," squeals Cali opening the door to Dylan, Len, Ivor, Jean and Joyce.

"Happy Birthday, Liberty," they all say, tottering into the room and crowding on the sofa.

Then it's cups of tea all round. And Hanna gets my dad busy with clearing the table and putting it away so there's space in the room for everyone to party. I'm amazed that he's not huffing and puffing and moaning like usual. He actually seems almost happy at having a job to do and he's behaving like an obedient and helpful little boy. He looks softer and less scary and I'd quite like to reach out and touch him or catch his eye and send a little parcel of love. But I'm too scared because I never know when he'll explode.

Dylan's made me a crazy card with cartoon aliens drawn all over them and gives me a half empty packet of chewing gum for a present. Len hands me a white handkerchief with little pink roses and the initial L embroidered in the corner.

"My late wife made it," he smiles. "Her name was Lily and she was a redhead too."

Ivor gives me a book all about bird watching, Jean gives me a box of yummy-looking chocolates and Joyce gives me a beautiful china teacup and saucer that's totally covered in a swirl of pink roses. Hanna hands me a bracelet made from beautiful green beads.

"Everybody ready?" she asks, turning off the lights.

Cali disappears into the kitchen. I know what's about to happen and I can't believe my luck. After a minute Cali appears holding an enormous chocolate cake that has eleven flickering candles on top and one sparkler in the middle to make twelve. The sparkler is showering the room with a thousand glittering stars that light up my smile.

"I made it," she smiles, "for my new best friend."

My heart bursts wide open with love and joy and if you could see what's going on inside you would definitely see a million flowers with their heads stretching up to the sun and a thousand butterflies fluttering with joy and a million swirls of happiness writing relief across my heart. Making a wish is easy. There's only one thing to wish for that would make my world more perfect than it is right now. I close my eyes and imagine my wish flying out into the universe, on its way to the great wish reader in the sky. I'd like to tell you what it is but I can't because told wishes don't come true.

Playing charades is a bit trickier than wish making. Some of the old folk are quite deaf so things get a bit confusing and not very successful at times. But I don't mind because to see my dad chuckling away with Hanna, like I've never seen him do before, is the best present I could ever have in the whole wide world. And he even joins in and does a charade and can't stop chuckling and chuckling when it all goes wrong. My dad is not the kind of dad to do a full-blown laugh; he'd be too shy for that. His laughter is let out in little chuckly spurts, like someone keeps shutting a door on it, afraid to let it all out at once, but still he's chuckling and that's new. It's like someone has opened a can full of fizzy life and given him a big drink of it and I feel all warm and safe inside. This is the strangest but most wonderful birthday party I've ever had in my whole entire life.

After charades the old folk start chatting away about the wonderful work Hanna does with the Community Action Scheme.

"She's a marvel," says Ivor to my dad. "Before she set it

up, us old folk could have rotted away and died in our flats for all anyone cared."

My dad's ears prick up and he starts asking all sorts of questions about the scheme and if they have premises and computers and lawyers and things.

"You must be joking," laughs Hanna. "This is a one-man band I'm running here," she smiles. "Nothing fancy, but it's essential in a place like this. People need help with all sorts of things and the council can only do so much."

Then Len starts up about the difficulty he's having with understanding how banking works these days and Jean says she can't understand some forms she's got to fill in and I can see my dad's brain moving into gear. He's plotting and planning and I wonder if he's getting interested again about having his fingers in some pies.

And we're all having the most perfect time until Dylan mentions *Bugsy Malone*. He's cracking and cracking his knuckles and Hanna tells him to stop it because she says it will overstretch his tendons and make his joints weak and then she suddenly squeals.

"Of course, I get it now, you're practicing for the school play, for *Bugsy Malone*. Are you in the play, Liberty?"

My tummy tightens and my second piece of chocolate

cake gets stuck in my throat. I need to stop them talking about *Bugsy*. I know I'm not actually going to be in it any more, but if my dad finds out that I'm getting involved in anyway at all that might distract me from my school work, I know he'll go completely mad. I start coughing and coughing, like I'm really having trouble with my cake and everyone's attention turns to me. And I think I've just about got everyone away from thinking about *Bugsy* when Joyce goes and makes things worse.

"Daaaarrrling," she says, handing me a sip of tea, "drink it down, you don't want to spoil that delightful singing voice of yours with all that coughing."

Chapter 18

It's dark here, really dark...

"Is there no end to your deception, Liberty?" my dad storms when we get back to our flat. "I don't believe it! If it's not one thing, it's another. You know how I feel about you getting involved with school plays and singing and time wasting activities like that, yet you persist in ignoring my wishes. And now you've gone and spoiled a perfectly pleasant evening, in fact the best evening I've had for years, believe it or not."

"I'm not doing the play, Daddy," I shout. "If you really want to know, I didn't want to sing in it, singing is Cali's and Joyce's thing. What I wanted was to play the violin. And yes, for your information, I have lied to you, Daddy, for years. Alice used to teach me the violin after her lessons. So I could do it, Daddy, it's true! It's only a little part, and I could manage it easily with a bit of help. But I know I'm not allowed, I know you hate it, I know you don't care about what I want to do with my life. If you really want to know, I hate you, I hate you and I wish I wasn't stuck in this stupid dump with you, and I never wanted Charles Dickens, not ever. I wish I could wash my hands of you too, because you're ruining my life. And I wish it was you that had died instead of my mum."

Before I know what I'm doing I've run out of our flat and slammed the door. I run down the stairs. It's cold out here, but I don't care. I don't care about anything any more; my life is rubbish, just like me. And now I've gone and said the worst thing ever to him. I saw him hold his cheek like my words had slapped him hard and now I can hear him calling after me, but I'm too scared to go back. I ignore him and just keep on running and running and running. I run past my school and towards the shops. My heart is beating fast in my ears; I'm out of breath and a stitch is sewing up my tummy so tight I can hardly breathe. I wish I could run for ever and ever and get far away from here.

The world is awake with evening sounds. Buses and taxis and cars are fighting for road space. The shops are fast asleep; they're empty and dark and waiting for morning when they'll burst into life and buzz with sales. The bars and restaurants are alive with fun, their windows glow yellow and warm and bright laughter is ringing from their doors. I'm hot, too hot, and my chest is about to explode with exhaustion. I can't breathe, but I don't care, I just keep on running and running and running until I nearly suffocate. I'm going to keep running and running until I can't run any more, until I collapse in a puddle on the ground. I run away from the shops and along the road that leads to the park. I run past the park and on and on to a place I've never been before. I'm pounding along a dual carriageway, cars are zooming into the night and a huge winding footbridge stretches over the road. I'm far away now, far away from home. And that's how I like it. There's no one to tell me what to do. I can live here for ever and ever like tramps do and never have to listen to my stupid old dad and his stupid demands ever again. I run over the footbridge and follow a footpath that leads to a canal. Danger is flashing through me like sirens, but I don't care; I don't care about anything any more.

I slow down. I'm thirsty and wish I had something to drink. It's dark here, really dark, except for the little ripples of water that have captured the light of the moon. My legs have turned to jelly and I'm cold. A chilly sweat creeps over my skin like a thousand tiny soldiers on patrol, shivering through me to my bones. There's no running left in me. I'm done, but I don't stop. I keep walking and walking because there's nothing else to do. I can't go home. Not now. Not ever. I've said too much and I wouldn't blame my dad for going crazy at me; I'd deserve it, I said the worst things ever and I hurt him. It's not his fault that he was the one who got to stay alive and I'm sure I'll get to like Charles Dickens in the end. And it was really kind of him to trust me with my great-grandmother's precious books. Shame paints itself over my skin and sticks like glue.

Someone's walking towards me. I can hear little bits of gravel crunching on the tarmac. I freeze and a moment later a big dog bounds towards me, nearly knocking me over. His owner whistles and the dog runs back. I hide in the shadows waiting for them to pass. I don't like it here. I want to go home, but I can't. I keep on walking. This is stupid; I can't go on for ever, not really. I wonder if Forrest

Gump felt like this when he started running? I wonder if he got to a point where he'd run so far that there was no turning back, even if he'd wanted to? I'm so busy with my thoughts that I don't see the gang in front of me. They've spread across the path so I can't get past.

"Excuse me," I say, trying to find a way through the crowd, "can I just get past, please."

"Yeh, right. Nah," says a big boy standing over me. "Why, what's your name?"

"Liberty," I say.

"You gotta pay, Liberty," laughs a girl with pink hair and bubble gum in her mouth. "Or else."

I move along the wall of kids, looking for a gap to squeeze through. But there's no gap. I turn to run back the way I came, but the gang closes in around me.

"Yeh, right, you gotta pay, girl," says a boy slurping beer from a can. "You got any money on you, right?"

'No," I say. I'm jangling with panic, "I'm sorry, really, if I had you'd be welcome to it."

"What else you got then, girl?" says a girl with a bottle in her hand. "You got a phone, iPod?"

"No," I say. "I don't have anything on me, really."

"You crack me up, Liberty," says the big boy. "No one

just goes out these days without nuffing in their pockets."

Then they start jostling and play fighting each other. I try to make a run for it, but bubblegum girl grabs hold of me. Fear prickles under my skin and freezes my brain. What should I do? What should I do? I'm numb and can't move.

"You can't escape that fast," she slurs, "we haven't finished with you yet. Fancy a quick dip in the canal, Liberty, or are you gonna empty those pockets of yours?"

"Please," I say, starting to cry, "please don't hurt me."

Then someone grabs me from behind, pulls me away from the crowd and says, "Liberty Parfitt, I do believe?"

Chapter 19

And then he's gone...

"Thanks for saving my life back there," I say.

My teeth are chattering with the cold so I move closer to Tyler to steal some of his warmth.

"You're crazy, you are," says Tyler, putting his jacket around my shoulders. "What do you think you're doing walking around dark places alone at this time of night? You're way too young for that."

"I had a fight with my dad," I say, "and I ran off. I can't go back home, though, not now."

"What's he gonna do, whip you or what?"

"No," I giggle, "he won't hit me. He'll just get cross."

"Then you got nuffing to worry about, have you? He'll

get over it, they always do. Nuffing's that bad."

Then somehow the whole story of my life starts tumbling out. It's raining and for a while we shelter in a late night café. Tyler gets us both a hot chocolate and we share some jellybeans from the machine.

"For your birthday," he smiles.

It's nice to have someone listen to me. And Tyler's good at it. He seems interested in what I'm saying and he doesn't try to tell me what to do, he just listens and listens and listens until there's nothing much left to say.

"Sounds like your old man's had a rough time of it," he says. "You too by all accounts. Come on, let's get you home."

And while we're walking Tyler tells me all about his life and about how he has to work at the tyre place after school just to help his mum take care of his younger brothers and sister, because there's not enough money to go round.

"Why is everyone so scared of you?" I ask.

"'Cause, when your old man beats you to hell and back like mine used to when I was young, you learn to stand up for yourself. No one's ever gonna touch me like that again, right, not ever. Day one at school I made my mark on the playground and that's how it's gonna stay. No one's getting to me."

Tyler walks me safely to our front door and waits with me until my dad answers. My heart is beating fast and my mouth's gone dry. My dad's face is white with worry and his eyes are red with tears.

"She's all right," says Tyler, "she's safe. Sounds like you two have got a lot of talking to do. Time to do it, I reckon, before it gets too late."

And then he's gone. For a while my dad and I stand just staring at each other. I think if we were in a film he'd hold his arms out and fold me into a warm, safe hug. But we're not in a film so he just sighs, mumbles something I can't hear, stuffs his hands deep into his jogging bottom pockets and slumps off back to the TV. We're obviously not going to take Tyler's advice and talk about things, so I slide into my room and take myself to bed.

I'm twelve years old and my life is ruined. If it hadn't been for Tyler tonight I might even have been dead, floating somewhere at the bottom of the canal and nobody would have cared. My dad probably wouldn't even have noticed if I'd never come home. I don't care about anything any more either – not even the stupid violin and stupid *Bugsy Malone*. There are more important things in the world to be worrying about. It's time to listen to my dad for once and pull my socks up and get my head down. Life isn't all about what I want and I need to get that firmly fixed in my head. Look at Tyler, he's only sixteen and he has to help take care of his family already. I've been living in la-la land and it has to stop, right now. I'm going to forget that I ever liked the violin and find some more sensible things to do with my time.

At midnight my phone beeps. It's a text from Alice.

Happy birthday to u, happy birthday to u, happy birthday dear Libby, happy birthday to u. Hope u had the best day ever. My mum's invited you for half-term. Please say yes! Love you Jellyhead. xxx

I close my phone and chuck it on the floor. Alice is living in la-la land too and she doesn't even know it and maybe she never will. Not until a truckload of rubbish gets dumped on her head and her dad's fallen into a pit of credit-crunch despair and she's turned into some sort of mad person that has fights and gets threatened by gangs. And that's never going to happen to Alice, because bad things never happen to her. Alice knows nothing, she's living in a safe little bubble where everything's happy and lovely and sparkly all the time. Sebastian's just as bad. He has no idea what's going on here and he never even bothers to call. If it hadn't been for Cali and Hanna and the old people, my birthday would have been totally one big, fat disaster. It's about time Alice and Sebastian grew up, just like I've had to.

My dad is grateful for my half-term invitation to Alice's house.

"I think it's for the best," he says, "give us both a bit of space."

I'm not so sure. I've *changed*, I can't be like Alice any more; I can't pretend everything's OK when it's so blatantly not. Alice and her mum want to come and pick me up but I'm too embarrassed for them to see where I live now. And it's not even that it's so bad any more, because there are nice people here, real people, it's just Alice wouldn't understand, not in a million years.

When my dad and I arrive at Alice's house I'm glad he made the effort to put on clean trousers, an ironed shirt and one of his smart office jackets that he hasn't worn in weeks.

"Henry," Alice's dad booms, shaking my dad's hand. "Good to see you, come on in. Liz has made some lunch, you will join us, won't you?"

My dad hesitates. I can tell that he'd like to just run away and hide in our crummy car and trundle back home, but he doesn't, he puffs himself up a little, paints a smile on his face and nods. "Super," he smiles, "really super."

I've forgotten what it's like to be in a soft, warm house full of cream carpets and massive snugly sofas and rugs. I've forgotten what it's like to have an icemaker in my fridge and to look inside and see it bursting full of food and to have an indoor heated swimming pool and a cinema room and my very own beach-themed en suite bathroom and glittering glasses and shiny silver cutlery and vases full of beautiful flowers. I can't believe that I took all this stuff for granted and that I thought that everyone lived like this. Not in a million years would I have imagined that people really lived in a flat like ours. I mean I saw them on the telly and stuff, but not in real life. The sight of it all twists in my throat like a knife and I have to swallow it down hard before it cuts me. My dad is holding himself taller, he's speaking louder, getting used to the fine crystal glass that is cradling his wine.

I feel strange around Alice. She seems younger than me now, or is it that I feel older? She hands me a birthday present and my tummy tightens because I know I'll never have enough money to buy her something back when it's her birthday. I hold the pink glittery parcel, scared to open it and see what's inside.

"A new phone, Alice!" I say, when I open the box. "You must be mad!"

"Well," she says, "it was Mummy's idea really, she thought it would be fun if we had matching phones, and she's put loads of credit on it for you, so you won't run out for ages."

All through lunch our dads go on about the credit-crunch and business stuff and I think my dad's enjoying getting his worries off his chest, just like me with Tyler. Dad also talks about Hanna and her Community Action Scheme and their lack of technology and all the old people who need help.

"Let's have a dig around in my office," says Alice's dad

to mine, "I'm sure I have a couple of old laptops I could donate to the good cause."

A few weeks ago my dad could have walked into a shop and bought ten brand new laptops without even thinking about it. But a few weeks ago he wouldn't have cared enough to do it.

Chapter 20

She pulls away from me and gasps...

When my dad leaves Alice's house he looks much more like his old self. He pats Alice's dad on the back, smiles and heads towards our crummy old car armed with the laptops for the Community Action Scheme and a pile of homemade goodies to eat from Alice's mum. Suddenly I miss him. I know I hate him a lot of the time, but I don't really, not deep down. I don't like the thought of him being in the flat alone with no one to grumble at. Sebastian's going off for half-term on some trekking thing for his Duke of Edinburgh Award Scheme, which means my dad will be completely alone for a whole week. I think if it had been possible he'd like to have stayed at Alice's house too. Just to have a rest from it all and feel the softness of our old life one more time.

Alice's mum packs us some picnic tea and sends us off for an afternoon ride. The woods are rich and heavy with swirling golden leaves that glow bright in the autumn sun. I'm riding Alice's spare pony, Kizzy – she's a gentle skewbald with a long cream mane. When we're clear of the woods and tumbling across the park I set myself free. Kizzy gallops faster and faster and faster and all of my troubles drop to the ground and get trampled by her hooves. I'm me again; I've come back to earth after being abducted by aliens and hidden in a dark cupboard for more than a hundred years and if I close my eyes it's as if nothing has changed. I am the same girl. I'm Liberty Parfitt with a Liberty Parfitt life. I can ride ponies every day and eat lemon cake whenever I want and ride in limousines and have tea at the Ritz with my granny and have money of my own to spend on useless things. I can lie on a beach for hours and order whatever I like for tea. I can fly in planes and shop for clothes and let my dad buy expensive food without worrying. But when I open my eyes my dreams fall like hail to the ground. Alice's face truly has no worries on it and my face has them written all over it in thick, black marker pen. Alice is smiling and laughing and gabbling on about Thea Quaddy and stupid, unimportant things. And I bet she's never even had one day where she's worried about money or ever met a sixteen-year-old who has to work to help his mum out or a girl with a million plaits in her hair that's never ridden in a limousine.

At suppertime Alice's mum is nosy, too nosy. She keeps asking questions about my dad and what happened to his business and about my new school and our home. She keeps fussing around me, like I need extra caring for or something, which is irritating, because I don't. Just because I don't have a mum of my own it doesn't give her the right to try and be my mother. It doesn't give her the right to try and take my mother's place. And anyway, I don't need her, I can manage alone; I have done for years.

I hate Thea Quaddy. Alice hasn't stopped going on about her and about all the fun stuff they've been doing since I left. She's invited Thea to go to Greece with her during the Easter holidays and she said that her mum would probably pay for me to go too if I wanted. But I don't. I don't want people to feel sorry for me and start paying for things for me all the time. I know I'm the poor girl now but everyone doesn't have to keep rubbing my nose in the fact. Soon I'll have to start saying thank you for breathing their precious rich air. My worry eczema pops up and starts bothering me again, so I hunt in my bag for my cream and slather it on my skin.

It's not until we go up to bed that I spot Alice's violin case. She's stuffed it in the corner of her room, probably hoping that her mum won't see it, which means she won't get nagged at about her music practice. While we're getting ready for bed my eyes keep being drawn back to it. I can't help it. It's too much knowing that it's there and not mine to play. My mouth is burning to ask Alice if I can take it out and have a go; better still if I could borrow it for *Bugsy Malone*, but I'm too angry with her, she's stupid and babyish now and she hasn't got a clue.

Lying in Alice's fresh, big double bed makes me feel sad and small. I curl up in a tiny ball to hide away from it all. All the softness and cleanness and safeness of her room pricks like a splinter that's stuck in my eye. I can't settle because a worry bug keeps shifting me around the bed not letting me get to sleep.

"My mum's been worried that your dad's going to get depression," Alice whispers into the night. "That can make people do weird things, you know. That's why she invited you here, to make sure you're OK. Thea Quaddy was going to come as well but my mum thought you probably needed some quiet time and some space to get used to things."

I turn over, move right to the edge of the bed, as far away from Alice as I can get, and pretend to be asleep. I don't care about Thea Quaddy but the word "depression" sticks in my ears. I've heard of it before but I don't really know what it is and I don't want Alice to know that. My dad is behaving weirdly, but so what? I don't want people talking about my dad's problems and getting all worried about us and involved in our lives. We can manage on our own, thank you very much. It's not their business; they should learn to back off.

It's the same the following day, Alice's mum takes us shopping and ends up buying me loads of things that I'd rather not have. She keeps asking if I have enough underwear and if my school shoes still fit. I know she's trying to be kind and everything and help my dad out, but we don't need their help, we're not a charity. And anyway, that's my granny's job and she still has plenty of money, she hasn't caught the credit-crunch disease yet and maybe she never will. And if Alice's mum doesn't stop soon I'm going to get the bus to a tattoo parlour and get them to tattoo the word "charity" across my forehead.

It's weird with Alice. It's like we're not equal any more. She keeps hopping around and showing me this new stupid dance thing that's going round the school. And she keeps telling me about the school skiing trip at Christmastime and how she and Thea Quaddy are going to share a room. She thinks she's so cool and cute and the only way I can shut her up is to tell her about me running away from home on my birthday and about being trapped by the scary gang. Her mouth drops open and for a wonderful moment she's speechless. Then she starts up again like a whirring old machine.

"Thea Quaddy said things like that might happen if you're living in a rough area like you do. People die you know," she says. "Gangs have guns and knives. It happens all the time."

Then I tell her about Tyler, the gang leader and how he's actually a really good friend of mine. She pulls away from me and gasps.

"You haven't got a knife, have you?"

"Don't be stupid," I sigh. "I haven't got a knife, Alice, but I know people who do. And it's not all terrible where I live, you know. Nice things do happen there too. And I have a new best friend called Cali and she is a *really* nice girl."

Chapter 21

This one last go...

By Thursday I've had enough of Alice. I can't believe she used to be my best friend, my most favourite person in the whole wide world. Now we have nothing in common. It's like I'm staying with a stranger. And I know she's itching to go to Thea Quaddy's on Saturday night for a Halloween party that I'm not invited to. I need to get home. The worry that's been niggling me and stopping me from sleeping at night since I've been here has turned into one big urge to get me back to my dad, and fast. The only problem is that I don't know how and first I just have to have a go on Alice's violin. It's been winking at me all week, inviting me to play, but I've been too cross with Alice to ask and she hasn't thought to offer. She's so obsessed with Thea Quaddy that she's probably forgotten everything we used to do together. I hate needing to play her stupid violin in the first place, but I do, I can't help it. I keep looking at it, trying not to want it, but it just teases me. The black case isn't so interesting at all, but I know of the treasures that await me inside. At breakfast I make a plan.

"Have you done your music practice, Alice?" I ask loudly in front of her mum.

Alice's eyes glare at me, telling me to shut up, but I won't.

"You probably have loads to learn for orchestra don't you, for the Christmas concert?" I smile.

"Liberty's got a point there, Alice," says her mum. "What with all the fun us girls have been having, I'd completely forgotten about music practice. I'm sorry, Liberty," she continues, "but you'll just have to amuse yourself for an hour while Alice does some practice. OK?"

"What did you go and say that for?" hisses Alice when we're sent up to her room, "you know how much I hate practicing."

"Sorry, Alice," I say, "I forgot. How about I do it for you, just to make it up to you and you can lie on your bed and read a book?"

Alice looks relieved and flops onto her bed.

I open the violin case slowly. My heart is racing with excitement. I know I've promised myself to stop this violin nonsense and get on with more important things, but I just need this one last go. It's impossible to describe the smell of a violin; it's something you have to experience for yourself. But I'm telling you, there's nothing else like it in this world. I breathe it in and my eyes soak up the shiny chestnut-coloured wood and the four little strings. Knowing it's the last time I'm ever going to play makes every little moment much more precious and I wonder if people feel like this when they know they're going to die. I wonder if my mum knew that the last time she played her violin was actually the last time ever? And I wonder where I was that day and what I was doing? I don't hurry. I pull out the bow, tighten it and rub the rosin up and down twelve times. When I'm ready, I pick up the violin and place it under my chin. Already I am lost. I haven't even started playing yet and I'm in a far away world where nothing else exists; the whole world has faded away and I am lost in the violin and under its spell. And Alice is too; she's stepped into the pages of a book and is lost in the world of its characters and what they're about to do next.

When I let the bow kiss the strings, glittering shivers run up and down my spine, like fairies dancing. The sad calling sounds echo through my brain and find a home in my heart. I was born to play this piece of wood and strings and if only I'd been allowed, my dad could have been so proud of me. He might have sent me little parcels of love in his smile or held my hand or taken me out for a special celebration lunch. I wish… But stupid God or whoever put me on this planet forgot to write this important piece of information on my nametag. So no one ever knew. But it doesn't matter. I've made a decision that enough is enough, if I can't get his attention the way I'd like to I'll just have to try something else. I'm going to give up worrying about the violin and start working hard at school so I can become something sensible, like a doctor or a lawyer – something that will help the world be a better place and make my dad smile again, maybe even at me. I wish I'd listened to him earlier on and given up on my stupid dreams.

After I've tuned up I play all the scales I know, like

they're the last delicious things I am ever going to eat. I chew them all slowly, like they're cream cakes or juicy mangoes or fresh raspberries with chocolate drizzle. Then I pull Alice's orchestral pieces out. These are like my main course. These are the fresh green salad or hot gravy roast. I'm a bit rusty, because it's been so long since I played, but still it sounds good and the music soars and swirls around the room, like medicine for my ears. As I play, every little muscle in my body relaxes, like I'm in a hot bubble bath of music. And all the worries in my brain are soothed away and will be washed down the drain when I've finished and it's time to pull the plug out. When I'm playing the violin nothing else matters, nothing else at all, and if heaven is like this then I know my mum is in a very happy place. Alice's mum calls from the hallway down below.

"Beautiful, Alice, I've never heard you play so well; you see – all those years of reluctant practice have paid off. I told you they would. Wait till Daddy hears you, he'll be so proud."

I let myself play one long last note. It's not part of a piece or anything; it's just my favourite note. I like it because it moves through my body and into my soul, into the part of me that nobody but me knows, into the part of me that makes me me. One small tear escapes from my eye and I stop. Then there's silence and I put the violin away.

"I need to go home," I say to Alice. "I don't want to make a fuss, I've got some birthday money, so I'll get the train. I just need to check the times on the internet and I need you to tell me where the station is, then I'll go."

"You can't get the train," laughs Alice. "I've never heard anything so ridiculous in all my life. Get the train! You're so funny, Libby."

"People get the train and the bus all the time," I snap. "Not everyone in this world has a car, you know and it's not funny, it's normal. You have to let me go."

"And if I tell my mum, who I know for sure won't let you go, what will happen then, Libby?" she smirks. "Are you just going to lash out like usual until you get your own way?"

Her words sting my ears and I can feel the heat rising up in me again, I can feel my rage about to spill out. But instead I take a deep breath, feel all the strength building up in me that I usually lash out and let it fill my body so I feel big and strong.

"One thing I've learned from all this, Alice," I say, "is that I don't have to lash out any more to get my own way, it doesn't get me anywhere anyway. But I do have to do what's best for me; I've spent my whole life doing what everyone else wants and now it's time to start taking care of myself. I'm not going to be pushed around any more, not by anyone."

"OK, OK, calm down," she says. "If you're that upset about it my mum will drive you back, or call your dad."

The night-time niggle that turned to an urge has now grown into panic and my worry eczema is burning my skin.

"Listen Alice, please! You have to trust me. I just need you to tell me where the station is and to divert your mum until I've gone. I'll be OK and I promise I'll phone you when I'm home. I have to go, now."

"Is it about the gangs?" she asks, opening her laptop.

"No, Alice," I say, "it's not about the gangs."

Chapter 22

Why didn't I get it before...?

While I'm checking for train times, I Google the word "depression" and I think Alice's mum is right. It says that depression is: *a low mood, a miserable feeling that goes on and on. People can get overly emotional and tearful or snappy and irritable. Depression can be triggered by all sorts of things such as someone close to you dying, losing your job or your home or by any shocking or traumatic events such as an earthquake, plane crash or disaster. Depression can make people want to withdraw from the world and stop going about their normal daily activities. In severe cases people can feel their lives are pointless and some can even think about harming themselves.*

And that's it. I suddenly know what my niggle is. Alice's mum is right, my dad has depression and I think he's got it bad. I throw my things into my bag, listen carefully to Alice's directions to the station and slip out of the front door without her mum seeing. I'm sorry if she'll think me rude; I probably am, but I know she'll just get in the way and slow things down if I tell her why I have to leave.

The air in the train is stuffy and hot and the urgency inside me is filling me up so much I think I might explode. And the train is taking so long. It stops for ages at every station and I wish it would just hurry up. The journey to Waterloo is supposed to take fifty-six minutes, but already it feels like I've been travelling for at least seven hours. Once I get to Waterloo station I have to get the underground train home. I haven't been on the underground alone before but I've done so many new things in the past few weeks, I don't even feel scared. And anyway, Cali does it all the time, so if she can do it, then so can I.

Why didn't I get it before? I mean, I knew there was something wrong with my dad's behaviour, but I've been so busy being angry with him for ruining my life that I haven't really thought about what's going on for him. He must feel terrible. No dad would disrupt their kid's life and make them live in a horrible place unless they had to. I'm so selfish. No wonder I'm such a disappointment to everyone. And I should at least have ignored his wishes and called my granny, even if it would have made him cross. Maybe with depression you lose sense of what you should and shouldn't be doing and my granny might have been able to put things right. I was silly to try and manage this alone, I should have asked for help. Twelve might be big, but not that big.

Alice sends me a text saying her mum's really worried about me travelling alone and that I *must* call her as soon as I get home. She says she's not going to call my dad because she doesn't want to overload him with any more worry and stress. And maybe it would have been a good idea for me to have thought about his needs a little more, before behaving irrationally and running off.

If she thinks she can control me by buying me a phone, then she's got another think coming. I told Alice once already that I'd call her when I got home. Why can't her busybody mum just trust me and leave me alone. I switch off my phone and throw it in my bag. I never even asked for a stupid phone anyway, especially not one the same as Alice's. I bet Thea Quaddy has one too.

Waterloo is busy. I hold on to my bag, push my way through the crowds and head for the escalator to the underground. It's confusing. Everyone is rushing about looking like they know where they're going. The man's voice on the loudspeaker echoes round the huge airy station making me dizzy. He's giving us all helpful information about trains and delays, but I can't understand what he's saying; his voice just disappears into the space and gets trapped on the ceiling. I wish I had someone's hand to hold on to, or even just Cali here with me to show me how it all works. I consider calling her and getting her to come and meet me, but that would waste time and time isn't something I have. I look on the map. All I have to do is get the Bakerloo line, which is the brown line, and then I'll recognise where I am and be home pretty quick.

The underground platform is crowded. Everyone's jostling, making sure they're ready to jump on the train when it arrives so they've got more chance of getting a seat. A great whoosh of air travels up the line, and then I can see the lights of the train shining through the dark tunnel. I'm nearly there. My insides are jumping up and down and the air above me feels heavy and tight. It's pressing down on my head like a heavy hat of gloom. Thoughts are flying round my brain like bats at night. I know something is wrong, but I don't know what it is. It's just a feeling I have to follow. If my dad's still OK I know he'll probably shout at me. In fact he'll be furious and mad that I've travelled home alone and been rude to Alice and her mum. But I don't care, so long as he's still alive he can do anything he likes, I won't mind. But if my dad has hurt himself like Google said he might, then I'll be the one to blame. I should have been paying better attention to his moods.

When I get back to our flats I don't feel very welcome. It's raining and grey and now I'm here I feel nervous. Maybe I'm being stupid, maybe there's nothing wrong at all and I'm making mountains out of molehills with the whole depression thing. It's quite likely, knowing me. My brain wants me to zoom up the stairs and into the flat fast but my feet are dragging behind. I don't know what I'm going to find.

"Hello, young'un," smiles Ivor, climbing into his old people's buggy thing. "See you Saturday afternoon?"

I nod and make my way up the stairs. Everything looks normal – well it would, I've only been away for a few days

– but something has changed. I can feel it sitting in the air like a dark monster, waiting to get me.

I knock at the door and wait. There's no answer and there's no telly sounds blaring away in the background. I lift the letterbox and call for my dad but there's no reply. My whole body is panicking, everything's on red alert. I bash the door again and keep on bashing harder and harder, but he doesn't come.

"Dad," I scream, "Dad! It's me, Liberty." My voice is screeching from deep in my tummy. "Please answer. Please be there, I'll never do anything wrong again, I promise. Just be there, please."

I wait a few more seconds but he doesn't come. The red alert starts flashing through my body, telling me to do something, making me run. I race upstairs to Cali's house. She'll know what to do, Cali always knows what to do in difficult situations, or if she doesn't, at least Hanna will. I bang on the door but there's no answer there so I lift up the letterbox and shout into the hall.

"Cali! Hanna!" I call. "Please answer, it's me, Liberty."

But no one answers, because there's nobody home.

A thought flashes through my brain like lightening, turning me into the wind, making me race back down the stairs, past the shops and behind the market to Tyre Right. A large stone is swishing in my tummy, making me sick. I can't believe I've let this happen. I'm so rubbish. I've failed again.

"Where's Tyler?" I scream to a man who's sweeping the garage floor.

"Calm down, missy, calm down," says the man, and then Tyler appears from behind a mountain of tyres.

"What's up, Liberty?" he says.

"Tyler!" I screech, running up to him. "I need your help, I think my dad's killed himself and I can't get into our flat!"

Chapter 23

No, I scream...

Tyler's face turns white. He drops everything, takes my hand and we start to run.

"He'll be OK," he puffs, getting out of breath, "I promise."

"But you can't promise that," I cry, "when you don't know."

When we get to our front door I knock again and there's still no reply.

"What shall we do?" I cry, clinging on to Tyler's arm.

"Well," he says, "we can call emergency services and wait ages for them to come, or I can break in right now and be done with it. These flats are easy enough to get into.

If it was *my* mum I was worried about, I know what I'd do."

"Break in," I say, "break in, Tyler, please, just get me in there, quick."

Tyler pulls something out of his wallet and fiddles with the lock. Then the door flies open and I start to rush in.

"Stay back," says Tyler, pushing me behind him. "I'll go in first. I don't want you to see nuffing that wouldn't be nice."

Then before Tyler even gets to the sitting room, my dad and Hanna arrive home, chatting and laughing together.

"Liberty!" he says. "What on earth are you doing here?"

"Dad!" I cry.

And then my dad notices that our front door is open and Tyler's inside.

"Hands up, young man. I recognise you. Thought you'd case up the joint did you, then take advantage of us being out?" my dad shouts, pulling his phone out of his pocket. "Step aside and put your hands up in the air."

"Dad," I shout, "Dad, no, leave him…"

"Stand back, Liberty," says my dad, "this boy's not safe, he might even have a knife. Stay close to Hanna."

"Tyler Brown," sighs Hanna, "I might have guessed you'd sink to this kind of behaviour."

"I've not done nuffing," Tyler pleads. "Believe me, tell 'em Liberty, I was only helping out."

"Helping yourself, more like," my dad blunders, dialling 999. "About time you got out and got yourself a job rather than thieving from innocent people's homes. Are you on drugs, young man?"

I snatch the phone from my dad's hand and stop the call.

"No," I scream, "listen to him, Dad. That's the problem round here, nobody listens! Tyler hasn't done anything and he's not on drugs; it was me. Alice's mum thinks you've got depression and I looked on the Internet and it said that people with depression can sometimes hurt themselves. So I got the train home because I thought you had. And then when I knocked at the door and you didn't answer I thought you were dead!"

I'm trembling, my body's turned to jelly and big sobs that have been sitting in my heart climb up to my eyes and flow over. I can't stop myself.

"Of course I'm not dead," says my dad, moving my wet hair out of my eyes, "I'm *never* going to kill myself and leave you, Liberty, however bad things get and I need you to trust me on that. Alice's mum was right, I have been depressed but that's normal when people have a sudden shock like losing a business and their entire fortune. It takes time to get used to all the new things and to find your feet again. But I'm working my way through it all, I promise, and I have no plans to leave you on your own. Hanna and I just went out for coffee to discuss the new plans for the Community Action Scheme."

And then Alice and her mum fly up the stairs looking like they've been running through ghosts at a hundred miles an hour.

"There you are," puffs Alice's mum, pulling me into a fussy hug. "We jumped in the car straight away, I was so worried about you. And you," she says, looking at Dad.

"Too much excitement for one day," says Hanna. "Why don't we all go up to mine and have a nice cup of tea?"

It's strange having Alice, Tyler and Cali, who's just got back, in the same room together. Tyler is looking awkward, like he doesn't really belong; he's too big for this room, too tall and out of place. Alice is looking down her nose at everything like she might get germs on her shoes and Cali's looking lost and confused, even though she's in her own house. I feel like a tube of superglue, trying to hold everyone together.

"I'm sorry, Tyler, for getting all dramatic and overexcited," I say. "I hope I didn't mess things up at work for you, again."

"Nah, you're all right, Liberty," he smiles. "I'm glad you feel you can count on me, not many folk do."

"Well," pipes up my dad, carrying in a tray of hot tea, "we can soon remedy that, Mr Tyler Brown. It's people like you we need to get this Community Action Scheme of Hanna's off the ground. You're young, you're strong and you've very obviously got guts and the young folk might listen to you. Can you use a computer?"

And it's like someone has switched a light on in Tyler's brain, like he's seen daylight for the first time in his life. He gets busy talking to my dad and Hanna about street crime and kids and drugs and things that would help improve everyone's lives. My dad and Hanna are all smiles with each other and smiling definitely wasn't something on the Google list for depression.

Alice's mum is sipping her hot tea as fast as she can. She's being polite but really I think she'd like to get back in her car with Alice, scrub them both off with baby wipes and get them both safely back to their perfect home.

"Well, I'm glad you're both safe and well, Henry," she smiles, "and I do apologise for letting Liberty escape the roost and travel alone."

"I'm learning a lot about Liberty myself," my dad winks, "and I'm coming to the conclusion that's she's just like her mother: wilful and wild. There's no stopping her you know."

And I know that it's time for me to apologise to Alice's mum for being so rude and causing her worry and time for me to give Alice a hug goodbye.

"I'm sorry I wasn't around for you when you needed me," says Cali, when everyone's gone and it's just her and me, together in her room. "I was up with Joyce, practicing *Bugsy*."

"It's OK, Cali," I say. "I was so scared he'd killed himself and it would have been all my fault. I rushed up to you first because you're good at sorting things out. You have a knack for it."

"That's what friends are for," she says. "Like Tyler says, Libs, you can count on your friends. Talking of which," she laughs, "d'you fancy going through my lines with me?"

Chapter 24

And now I'm confused...

It's easy giving up the violin. I'm putting my head down at school, getting on with my school work and not even thinking about the violin one tiny bit. After all, it's only a violin, it's not the end of the world or anything.

It's the beginning of December and I've had almost one whole month without getting into trouble at home *or* at school, which is a big relief for me, for my dad *and* for Mrs Cobb.

"I'm glad to see you're settling in at last, Liberty Parfitt," she says, passing me in the playground.

When Cali, Dylan and everyone else are busy rehearsing *Bugsy Malone*, I take myself off to the library to work alone. I've decided to become a paediatrician when I grow up (that's the long word for children's doctor) which means I need to work really hard at science. Dr Johnson, our science teacher, thinks I can make it and although science is not my best subject, I'm starting to understand it more and more. I'll have to do A levels after my GCSEs and then go on to medical school after that to train. I know it's a long way off *and* it will be a lot of hard work, but my dad seems much, much happier with me now I've made myself a plan.

My dad seems happier with himself too. He still bursts into tears sometimes and sometimes he still sneaks into my room at night and talks to Lissy in the dark and falls asleep on the end of my bed. It's a bit spooky. He's either talking to a ghost or talking to me but getting my name quite wrong. But he's not watching so much telly any more or drooping about the place. He's washing and shaving every day again and wearing proper clothes. He spends lots of time with Hanna and Alice's dad's laptops trying to do fundraising for the Community Action Scheme. They're trying to get the Council to give them an office to use and enough funding so that my dad and Hanna can get paid to work full time. They have all sorts of ideas to help the old people and single parents and sick people and they're trying to set up places for teenagers to go at night, to have fun, instead of hanging out on the streets. Tyler's getting really involved with this and is even thinking of training to be a youth worker when he finishes school.

"Your old man's all right, Liberty," he says. "I could have made something of myself if I'd had a dad like yours."

I haven't heard from Alice since the day I thought my dad had killed himself and I feel a bit guilty about not calling her, especially when it was her mum that bought me the phone. But then she hasn't called me either. So I'm not sure what to do. I mean, she was my best friend for years, but now we're just so different. I'd quite like to ask my dad's advice, but that's never going to be possible because we still don't talk. Well, I mean, obviously we do talk about things like what we're having for dinner and what you have to do to become a paediatrician, but we don't talk about important things like how we're feeling. We've never even mentioned the night I ran away and got trapped by the gang, or about me getting panicked about my dad killing himself and running off from Alice. After we'd finished having cups of tea with Hanna that day we just came back to our flat and carried on like nothing serious had happened. And I never ask him about how he's feeling or about his late-night crying visits to my room when he sleeps on my bed. I don't like it, but he's not really doing any harm and if we talked about it, I wouldn't even know what to say. In our flat those topics of conversation have a big, "Don't go there" sticker stuck right on top of them. I think my dad is the type of person who likes to brush his problems and worries under the carpet and pretend they don't exist. Or maybe he really has washed his hands of me and just doesn't care any more.

Cali and I still help the old people on Saturdays. We still read the paper to Joyce and have tea and cake but I always make an excuse to leave when they get the big fat book of musicals out. My dad has made his feelings loud and clear about me getting involved in that kind of thing and if I want a peaceful life then I just have to listen and do as he says. Maybe, when I actually get to become a paediatrician, he'll send me a little parcel of love that will land like glitter on my smile, just like he does with Sebastian. That is a day I'm wishing for, a day where I can make my dad proud.

It's annoying because every time we have a class music lesson Mrs O always says, "Remember, Liberty, that violin part in *Bugsy* is yours if you can find yourself an instrument. There's no one else to do it, so if you don't turn up, we'll just have to use the CD player instead."

I wish she wouldn't keep saying it. I wish I'd never asked her in the first place. She just needs to shut up about it and let me get on with more important things. Then, when she tells us she's going to start up a choir so we can tour the country and try and win competitions for our school, she causes even more trouble between Cali and me.

"Come on," says Cali, "let's join! At last The Grave is doing something exciting. It'll be brilliant!" Then she wiggles her bum and says, "Hollywood's not gonna know what's hit it when I arrive on the scene! And remember," she taunts, "champagne, parties, limousines!"

And of course a little part of me would love to join the choir, but I don't want to upset my dad again. I need to stick to my plan.

"No," I say, "I don't care about limousines, Cali, and I don't care about the choir. I'm going to do something important with my life. I'm going to be a paediatrician, remember, and I don't think you have to be good at singing to do that. Unless you're the kind of paediatrician that sings to the children on her hospital ward."

"Oh, come on," she says, "it's just for fun, Libs. You don't do anything fun any more. It's just work, work, work, with you and it's boring! If you're not going to join the choir, you should at least get involved with *Bugsy* in *some* way, I don't know, backstage or ticket selling or something."

"Well you were the one who thought this school was stupid and that no one ever wanted to work hard and learn anything and now I've given up messing around and I'm trying, you're still not happy. You can't have it both ways, Cali," I snap.

"Of course you can," she says, "it must be possible to work hard *and* have fun."

And now I'm confused.

"Well, you don't have to live with my dad," I sigh. "He hates me doing that sort of stuff and you know it. Just go to choir yourself, Cali and leave me out of it. OK?"

"Yeah, I might just do that," she persists. "But don't you think it's weird that your dad won't let you? I mean it's not like it's harming anyone is it? I mean no one's gonna die if you join a choir? It's ridiculous and what's worse is that you're doing what he says and you haven't even asked him why. You don't even know what's at the bottom of all this. It doesn't make sense."

"Yes, well," I gruff, "there's a lot of stuff in this world that doesn't make sense, Cali, and we just have to get used to it. If your life was anything like mine, then you might understand."

Chapter 25

I'm not feeling fine...

I'm busily amusing myself in the library. I have to colour in a worksheet picture of a human eye. The human eye is quite fascinating and I'm learning all sorts of important things like the fact that the coloured part of your eye is called the iris. The iris controls how much light enters your eye. And the whole inside of your eye is filled with jelly, which is actually called the vitreous humour and it's that bit that gives our eyes their golf-ball shape. Learning about eyes is going to be more useful for someone who wants to be an optician when they grow up, as opticians really need to understand eyes. But I guess that as most children do have eyes, it will be very useful for me when I'm in a hospital being a paediatrician as well.

Anyway, I'm merrily enjoying my colouring in when Dylan bursts into the library wearing very strange clothes.

"Libs," he shouts, "you have to come quick, it's Cali."

"Shhhh," hisses the library lady, "in case you've forgotten, young man, this is a library, it's a quiet area for study, *not* the playground."

"What's happened?" I whisper, packing up my things. "What's going on? Is she all right?"

"You just have to come, Libs, and fast."

I follow Dylan and we run past the music centre and make our way to the drama hall.

"What is it? Dylan, tell me! And why are you wearing those stupid clothes?" I say.

"Just in time, Libs," he smiles, settling me down on the drama studio seats. "Listen to her, she's amazing."

So I do. There in the middle of the stage, with the lights shining on her, is Cali.

"It's the dress rehearsal for *Bugsy Malone*," he whispers, running off to join everyone on stage. "You've missed some of it, but I couldn't let you miss this."

Cali is sitting on a stool; she's wearing a 1930s dress

with a funny old hat that's pulled down low. The lights soften, a lonely piano starts up and then Cali breaks out in song.

"I'm feeling fine," she sings, *"Filled with emotions, stronger than wine, they give me the notion…"*

The little army of soldiers are marching up and down my neck again making my hairs stand on end. Her voice is amazing! Everyone on stage and everyone sitting with me is silent. We're all just listening to her. I'm even worried about breathing because I'm afraid of breaking her spell. Cali always sings brilliantly, but this is different. Her voice is slicing through the air, filling every corner of the studio with a clear silvery light, filling me up and up with emotions that I do not want to have.

I want to be on stage too! What did I do? Why did I give up on myself? I want to be playing the violin or in the chorus or a lady in the bar, or even backstage. I want to be anything, just anything, anything, anything! I hate this! I hate myself! I hate my dad! I hate stupid Dylan and I hate Cali and Blousey Brown! I wish I could get up and leave and go back to my colouring-in or leap on the stage and just burst into song. Why did Dylan have to disturb me and upset me? Why can't everyone just leave me alone to get on with working hard so I can become a paediatrician? I do want to be a paediatrician, I do! I do! I do!

I get up to leave, then sit down again, then get up again, then sit down. Mr Forrest makes firm eyes at me, telling me to do one thing or another. So I start to leave and then I sit. I'm staying. It's Mr Forrest's fault that I'm here. If I had my way I'd just get up and leave. Why didn't I just lie to my dad and do *Bugsy* in secret? He never had to find out, I've lied to him before.

I'm not feeling fine, Cali and it's all your fault. When they sing the song, 'So You Wanna Be a Boxer', I feel even worse because there's a golden boy inside me too, well not exactly a boy, but there's a golden girl inside me, waiting to become who I am. The words in the song that go, "*So you might as well quit, if you haven't got it*" punch me in the face. Am I a quitter? Have I quit? I haven't quit anything. I've made up my mind what I'm going to be and I'm going to be a paediatrician and that's that. Sorted! The whole song stirs up a mountain of trouble inside me. Like there's a boxing match going on in my body and I don't know if I'm winning or losing. This musical is rubbish, it's stupid, stupid, stupid and I'm not even going to come and see the real performance.

If Mr Forrest didn't keep glaring at me with his googly eyes, I'd just get up and leave and never come back. But I can't, he's forcing me to stay glued to my seat until the very boring end. The last song is more rubbish than them all. I don't even want to listen to the lyrics but they keep wriggling into my brain, making themselves at home without my permission.

Suddenly the whole stage breaks out into one massive splurge gunfight. Dylan's gone on and on about this scene for days. He's totally in love with it. Everyone is completely covered in boring custard goo and singing together with smiling faces. It looks kind of fun… but not as much fun as the food fight I started in the dining hall. That was real fun. This is for babies.

After school Cali has another boring play rehearsal, but I don't care because I don't want to hang out with her tonight anyway. I have a science project I want to finish before the weekend, so I'm going to get my head down and do that.

"It's good to see you working so hard, at last," smiles my dad when he's making our dinner.

I'm sitting at the kitchen table drawing pictures of cells.

You wouldn't believe how fascinating they are. There's a mini world going on inside every single, teeny-weeny, microscopically small, cell in our body and that's a lot of cells because the average body has between 50 and 75 trillion of them. That's obviously too many to draw, so I draw one big one, carefully label it and then do a mass of tiny dots so it looks like there might be at least 50 trillion of them on my page.

"You're following in Sebastian's footsteps and getting interested in science," he says. "He'll be home for Christmas soon, so you two will have a lot to talk about."

I nod, but deep inside I know that I'm not really interested in talking to Sebastian about science. For one thing, he knows so much and once he gets started on it he can talk and talk until my whole body explodes with boredom and my ears can't focus any more on what he's saying. And for another, I'm scared that Sebastian might spot the fact that I'm just one big fake head and spill my secret to dad.

Chapter 26

You could have been anything...

I've been lying in bed for ages and I can't get to sleep. I pick up the book of poems that Matron gave me, but throw it down because the book reminds me of my old school and my old school reminds me of Alice and thinking of Alice makes me feel guilty. I should phone her, but then she could just as easily phone me. I try starting one of the Charles Dickens's books called *Little Dorrit*. I like the name and how it feels in my mouth, "Little Dorrit." I'm hoping I'll start reading and get lost in the wonderful world of Charles Dickens. But the first paragraph is going on about a blazing sun in France and that reminds me of our French house with the pool and blue shutters and our vineyard and our boat. It reminds me of things I'd rather not think about. Things I'd rather brush under the carpet with my feelings.

My arms and legs are fizzy and itchy and I can't get comfortable. My bed is too soft and my pillow's too hard. I kick my duvet off for a while to cool down, and then pull it back on when I get too cold. I wish the night would disappear and be eaten up by the day. There's more to do in the day. At night there's just nothing and nothing and nothing but more night, more dark, and more eerie shadows creeping on my walls.

The stupid *Bugsy Malone* songs keep wriggling through my brain, trying to find a resting place for the night. They're like my dad looking for the warm patch at the end of my bed. They keep moving and moving, getting more and more restless and more and more annoying, wriggling and wriggling, like a puppy in its bed. The worst song was the last one with the splurge gunfight and the words keep chugging around my brain like my old Thomas the Tank Engine train, without ever stopping at the railway station.

"*You could have been anything that you wanted to be, and it's not too late to change. You could have been anything that you wanted to be, you could have been anything that you wanted to be.*" It just keeps going round and round and round, making me want to scream. "*You could have been anything that you wanted to be, and it's not too late to change.*"

I know I could be anything that I want to be, I shout in my head. *But I can't, so shut up, will you?*

I wish I could talk to Cali, but she won't understand. She doesn't know what it's like to have to do stuff you don't want to do, just to keep your dad happy. If I could go and see Tyler, he would understand. He'd just listen and encourage me to make up my own mind. I switch my bedside lamp on and pull on some clothes. If I leave now I'd find Tyler, go for hot chocolate while he listens to my troubles and be back before my dad even notices I'm gone. Then another *Bugsy Malone* boxing match starts up inside my body, bashing and punching. I want to go, but I know I shouldn't. But I want to. But I shouldn't. Mr Forrest's googly eyes are sitting in my head staring at me again, telling me to do one thing or another. And then I remember the cold and the gang and the canal and the fact that Tyler would go mad at me if he found me out late at night on my own again. I throw off my clothes, climb back into bed and sigh.

It's so unfair; everything in my life is so unfair.

I still can't get to sleep, so I get up and make myself some hot chocolate. My dad's snoozing in his own bedroom for once, without prowling into mine, so I decide to get up for a while and enjoy some peace and quiet. I'm just getting cosy on the sofa, trying out Charles Dickens's *Dombey and Son* – I like the word "Dombey" – when I spy something out of the corner of my eye. Tucked between two books on the bookshelf is a CD. The bottom of it is sticking out like someone forgot to put it away properly. In most homes this wouldn't be a problem. I mean, in most homes you probably wouldn't even notice a randomly sticking out CD. But in our home it's sticking out like a bright blue police siren, flashing in the night. I check my dad's still sleeping and close the sitting room door. My dad doesn't own CDs. I don't own CDs. I just have my secret iPod like I know Sebastian has in his dorm at school. It's probably no big deal. Hanna probably leant it to him or something not realising that we don't actually have a CD player to play it on. Then I spy one of Alice's dad's laptops on the floor. Has my dad been listening to music on the laptop? My heart jumps. It would be amazing if my dad started letting us listen to music. He might even… no, Liberty, put that thought away, you don't even want to play the violin any more.

I check on my dad one more time to make sure I haven't woken him then quietly pull the CD off of the shelf.

The picture on the front is a painting of a woman on a golden chair wearing a black evening dress, playing a violin. A violin! Her arms and face are pale and her hair is red. Her hair is red and curly, like mine. Then I notice the writing at the bottom saying, "Lissy Parfitt: Vivaldi: The Four Seasons." Lissy Parfitt! Lissy Parfitt! Lissy Parfitt! Lissy is the person my dad keeps talking to in the night and Parfitt is our surname. Then the fireworks go off in my brain. Who is Lissy Parfitt? My brain is exploding inside my skull. I turn the CD over to look at a photo on the back and I can't believe my eyes. Staring out at me is a photo of my mum. It's the same as the only one I've ever seen of her. But her name was Elizabeth, not Lissy! Unless… of course… Lissy was her nickname? My dad has been talking to my mum in the night! I stroke the photo of my mum, and let her name roll around in my mouth. Lissy… Lissy… Lissy. My heart is booming in my ears. I know my mum was obsessed with playing the violin but I didn't know that she'd made a CD. It looks like my mum was famous and if I hadn't found this CD I might never even have known.

The big question that's spinning around my head now is if my *dad* listens to this, why has he never played it to *me?* Why hasn't he shared her with me? Cali's right, I need to do some detective work and try to get to the bottom of the story of my mum. I have a right to know what happened.

I check on my dad one more time. I'm panicked that he'll wake up and find me with the CD, then my life just wouldn't be worth living. But it's OK, he's fast asleep, snoring and twitching. I close his bedroom door, grab my headphones from my room, close the sitting room door and turn the laptop on. My hands are shaking as I pull the CD from its case and slip it in. It takes a while, then the music streams into my ears and I'm whisked far away to violin heaven. The sounds are weaving and playing and leaping and running. Like bubbling streams in spring and lambs skipping and flowers budding and the sun shining brightly, breaking out of the gloom of winter. Then, like a bird singing above the orchestra, a solo violin part soars, like an angel, straight up to the sky and swoops back down and into my heart.

When the summer part of the CD comes, I'm floating down on to a soft pillow of grass. Wildflowers are tickling my nose. Butterflies and birds are fluttering in the breeze and I'm breathless with the delight of it all. When it's time for autumn, I'm lying on a golden bed of leaves. They're swirling down to the damp ground below and a sad feeling creeps in as the world slowly moves its way, closer and closer towards the darkness of winter. When winter comes, the world is bleak and cold with frozen ice and snow.

I can't believe my *mum* actually played these amazing sounds and worse still, I can't believe that my *dad* has kept them from me for so long. And if he's hidden *these* for so long, I wonder what else might be hidden right under my nose?

Chapter 27

I'm getting warmer...

I wake in the morning and stare out at the day with new eyes.

After listening to my mum playing the violin last night, I can never go back to how I was before. Her magical sounds soothed and glittered through me and found a cosy home right under my skin and if I touch my arm or my hand or my leg I can feel her right here with me. Like she's never been gone and I've never been without her, like someone's sewn more stuffing into me and puffed me up like a lovely soft cushion. I wish I was brave enough to tell my dad the truth about my discovery and ask him why he's kept this secret for over ten years. I mean, what's the point?

Cali's right, why wouldn't he want me to know about my mum?

It's Saturday and at breakfast time he's almost smiling.

"I'm busy with Hanna today," he says. "The council have finally found us an office for the Community Action Scheme. It's a shell of a building along the canal, a bit grotty by all accounts, but we've got a grant to do it up, so it's a good start. Will you be all right on your own for a while?"

"That's great news, Daddy," I say, really meaning it.

I watch him moving about the kitchen, buttering toast and making coffee and I wonder where he keeps his secret. It's not obvious in his face or his eyes or in the way he stands and if you bumped into him in the street there would be no way you could ever tell. But after so many years of practice I guess he's got very good at hiding it by now.

"Don't worry about me, Dad," I say. "I'm visiting the old people with Cali this afternoon and I have some homework to get on with this morning. I won't get into any trouble, I promise."

I don't really want to visit the old people today. Tonight is the first performance of *Bugsy Malone* and I know Cali's going to go on and on and on about it, nonstop, for ever and ever. "Hollywood, here I come," she'll say, wiggling her bum, "blah, blah, blah." I'm tired of listening to her. I mean, I do hope she gets to Hollywood, but there are other things in this world to talk about as well.

When my dad leaves the flat my tummy turns into a food blender and churns my breakfast into mush. I know what I have to do, but I also know that what I have to do is wrong, *very* wrong. Rummaging through people's private property isn't fair, even if it is a member of your own family. Trust and privacy are important. But surely finding out about your past is important too?

I check outside to make sure my dad has left the building and spot him and Hanna walking out through the car park towards the canal. I'm pleased he's made a friend. Only a couple of months ago my dad wouldn't even have noticed Hanna in a crowd, let alone spoken to her and become her friend. Having Hanna around has definitely helped him come out of his depression and it's brilliant that my dad's helped Hanna get her project off the ground. I know the whole credit crunch thing has been hard for my dad, but I think in lots of ways it's changed him, for the better.

I creep into his bedroom. I know he's not here, but I still feel scared. My eyes are all over the room, looking for something, but I'm not sure what. I search through the piles of papers and the stuff stacked up in the corners but there's nothing there. I wish I had X-ray vision so I could see what's in the dusty boxes and suitcases and trunks without actually having to open them, but I don't, so I really don't have any other option.

I pull one of the boxes from the pile and place it on the floor. I'm not sure if I'm more scared to find what I'm looking for or truly more scared that I won't. I lift the flap open and peer inside. Staring up at me is Molly, my old rag doll. I can't believe she's here! I give her a kiss, sit her on my lap and dig deeper inside. There are so many treasures I haven't thought about in years. My baby doll's here, my first ever Barbie and my entire Sylvanian Family collection. In an old shoebox I find my Thomas the Tank Engine track and trains and tucked inside an old top hat is my Sleeping Beauty dress. There's a heart-shaped tin filled with all my beautiful baby jewellery and tiny treasures and there's loads of Sebastian's stuff here too. There's his magnifying glass, his magic set, his collection of Dr Seuss books and a mini baseball glove he had when he was five.

My dad must have saved all this stuff when he cleared out our houses. I could have imagined my dad throwing it all in the bin, not saving stuff, but he didn't, it's all here. I wonder why he hasn't shown me before? It's wonderful being surrounded by it all. I almost feel like I'm back in our London house playroom and that at any moment Sebastian's going to burst through the door and ask me to play. And then we're going to tumble into the garden and one of our nannies will have prepared us a wonderful picnic feast with ice cream and strawberries. Then at night-time I'm going to snuggle up safe in my big brother's bed and he's going to tell me funny jokes until we're laughing so much our faces will crack in two. I touch all of my treasures one by one and then put them carefully back in their cardboard nest.

Box number two is full of boring things like headphones, computer leads, old cameras and all sorts of stuff that I'm definitely not looking for. But I rummage through, just in case. At a first glance, the third box looks like it's just full to the brim with a pile of old clothes. I rummage through them anyway and under some jeans and a stripy grey jumper, I discover the most beautiful dresses I have ever seen. I pull them out one by one and find a green one totally covered in sparkling sequins, a blue one covered in tiny shimmering pearls and a purple one with silver threads sewn through that glitter in the light. Things in this flat are getting weirder and weirder by the minute. Why has my dad got dresses in his room? I hold the purple one up to myself, itching to try it on. I can't resist it. I pull off my clothes and slip it on. Its smooth silkiness slides on to my body, rippling like waves on a glittering purple sea. I stand in front of the mirror. It's only a little bit too big for me and I feel like a real princess getting ready for the ball.

I search in the bottom of the box and find a man's shirt with a pointy-up collar and black bow tie. Now these obviously belong to my dad, because he wears things like this to smart dinners, which means... maybe the dresses belong to my mum? My tummy leaps into my mouth. I hold the green dress up to my face and breathe it in, hoping to smell something of her, hoping for a clue. Did my mum really wear these clothes? I have to hurry; my dad will be back soon.

I pull an old brown suitcase from the top of the trunk pile and struggle to lift it on the bed. It's covered in stickers from all over the world. I try to open it but it's locked. I wiggle the catches just to make sure, then search in my dad's drawer for the key that I can't find. I shake the case and something heavy thuds inside.

The big brass catches on the first trunk aren't locked. I click them free and the huge lid creaks as I open it up. There's stacks of stuff inside. Piles of it! Excitement is galloping through me. I'm getting warmer; I know that I am. First I find a stack of magazines all about the world of classical music. I flick through a few and am about to put one down when a picture of my mum stares out from the page. I can't believe my eyes because she's wearing the purple dress! Exactly the same one as I'm wearing right now! The article is all about my mum and some concert she was playing in Vienna. I'm dying to read the whole thing, but I know I'm getting warmer and warmer and I just have to keep on going. Next, I find some more CDs. I can't believe it, there are so many of them, piled up in the corner of the trunk. Most of them have pictures of my mum on the front wearing a beautiful dress and sometimes her hair is long and sometimes it's short. It feels strange having her peering at me through the plastic case. It's like she's looking at me but can't actually see me. I give her a little wave, hoping she might leap out and join me, but she doesn't, she just keeps smiling and smiling and I start to feel spooked. I grab the laptop from the sitting room and put a CD on called *Air on G String* by a man called Johann Sebastian Bach. I wonder if Sebastian was named after him?

Chapter 28

The sound of two violins...

After *Air on a G String*, I put on a CD with music written by a man called Tchaikovsky. The piece is called 'None But the Lonely Heart' and the title is true. It's like the greyest day in history and the saddest face in the world and the lost little doggy, sitting alone in a boat that has washed for ever out to the roughest sea. I'm washed out to sea and there's no lifeboat in sight. I lay back on my dad's bed, close my eyes and let the music wash over me, wave after wave after wave.

Seeing pictures of my mum's face all around me, and feeling the silkiness of her beautiful dresses, makes me wish I could remember her. But however hard I try to rummage around in my brain looking for a memory, even just a teeny-weeny one. I don't have any luck. Having her things here makes me realise what I've missed. I'd like to be able to cuddle her and eat with her and go to the shops and do normal stuff like that. If I could have her back I wouldn't even mind having an argument with her. I'd like anything at all. Just to hear her voice say, "Liberty, I've had enough of your mess, now will you please clean up your room?" Or, "Liberty, can you go and get ready for bed please?" I don't even know what her voice was like. When your mum's not with you, it's not the special things you miss or the exciting things, it's the everyday things, the normal things. It's the things that make you feel close to her.

For a moment, I imagine my mum is alive and real and in this room with me, playing her violin. She's playing our special tune, the one that she plays me every night before I go to sleep. Her music is kissing my cheek goodnight and tucking me in so I'm safe and warm. Then just before I fall asleep she pulls me up, out of my bed and we dance around my room to a CD that she's just recorded in New York. She loves me so much that she can't bear it when I go to sleep, because she says that she misses my smile.

If a glittering fairy godmother would magically swoop

out of the sky, land in my room and give me one wish, it would be to have my mum back for just one day. Just to see her and have her see me one more time. I mean I've grown up so much since she last saw me! I've changed from a chubby baby into a twelve-year-old girl and I wonder if I passed her in the street if she'd even remember me. If I could have her back for just one day, then maybe I could let her go again. Maybe she would play the sad violin music and fly high up and up and away. And we might cry and stretch our hands out for each other, wanting to stay near. But she'd say, "Liberty, I'm so sorry I have to go. I want to stay with you a million times over and if I had just *one* wish, then *you* would be my wish come true. Dying is a part of life, just like being born. And I'm so sad that I had to leave you before you were all grown up and ready for such a thing. But never forget that I love you, always and always, for ever and ever and if ever you need me you'll always find me tucked safely away in your heart and glittering under your skin." I stroke my freckly arms to feel her and when I hold my hands together it's as if I'm holding hers.

I shuffle through the CDs deciding what to put on next, when I see one called *Bach Double (Concerto for Two*

Violins) and my eyes nearly pop out of my head when I see a photo on the front of not only my mum, but my dad as well! And he's wearing the shirt that I found in the box with the black bow tie! I put the CD in the laptop and listen. The sound of the two violins swirling and leaping and dancing all over me makes me dizzy. I stare at the photo and can't believe my eyes. My dad hates music! He won't even listen to the radio! And he can't even play the violin… can he? He hates the violin! He won't even let *me* play!

I rush back to the trunk and my eyes find so much more inside. There are trophies and faded dried flowers and thousands of "Good Luck" and "Well Done" and "Missing You" cards from my dad to my mum and my mum to my dad and bits of ribbon and stacks of sheet music from every composer you could ever imagine. Right at the bottom are a pile of programmes from concerts all over the world. Most of them are covered in my mum's name, but on some of them is my dad's. My dad has played in Russia and Paris and London and Australia, and even on TV! I leaf through the magazines and find out more and more about my past. Like the fact that my mum and dad met each other at music college when they were only eighteen and that they had a "passionate and volatile relationship", whatever that means.

Angry feelings start bubbling inside and they bubble right up and turn into fat angry tears that make little salty rivers run down my cheeks. I want to hold all of these treasures I've found and keep them safe for ever and yet at the same time I want to tear them all up and throw them in the bin and forget I ever found them. How did my dad think he was going to keep this massive secret from me for ever? And why would he even want to? I have a right to know! And does Sebastian know? And why didn't my granny tell me? That's why he keeps her away from me as much as he can. That's why they don't get on. It all makes sense now. That's why he never wants her around and never wants her to get involved in anything; he's been scared that she'll let the cat out of the bag. But she never would. I've asked her about my past so many times before and she never told me any of this stuff. Why has everyone in my life been keeping such a big fat secret from me? Did my dad really plan to lie to me for the whole of my life?

The *Bach Double* finishes and I put on a CD called *Beethoven: Romance for Violin* and listen while I pull the empty trunk on to the floor and open the last one underneath. In it are a million photo albums of my mum and dad and Sebastian. I hate Sebastian; why does he always have all the luck? The three of them are all over the world, smiling and laughing together. And there are all these other people in the albums as well that I don't even know.

I turn the music up as loud as it will go, so it's crashing through my ears, blocking out the world and look through the photo album pages one by one. I'm not anywhere. There's no sign of me. No one would even know that I was a part of this family too. It's not fair! I'm just about to put them all back and close the lid when I spy a pink photo album hiding in the bottom of the trunk. I pull it out and blow off the dust. On the front of the cover in shining sequins are the words, "Liberty, my darling girl". I touch the sequins with my finger and trace the words and wonder if it was my mum who stuck these on? I open up the album and there I am! I'm so small and cute and my hair is so red and there's Sebastian and my mum and dad all smiling together. And there I am again sitting up with a toy in my hand and there I am laughing with mushy food dribbling down my face. And there I am and there I am again and again until the last photo at the end of the book, which is of my dad and me. It's my first birthday, so my mum was already dead, and he's holding me up to blow my birthday candles out. I look so smiley and happy; I couldn't help it, I didn't know that such terrible things had happened. I lie back on the bed and hold the album tight. I'm so tired and angry and happy and sad from it all that I close my eyes and let the music take me away. And I'm just floating to a place where I think I can see my mum waving to me and smiling when…

"Liberty!" my dad booms. "Whatever are you doing?"

Chapter 29

And then you came along...

I freeze. My dad is towering over me. His face is white. I'm wriggling around in my mum's dress, trying to climb out of it but I can't so I let it fall back down around me and leap up and scrabble about in the messy piles of CDs and magazines and photographs and cards, quickly trying to put them all back without spoiling them. I wish more than anything that I could climb into the trunk and close the lid on myself and never come out again. I promised that I wouldn't get into trouble today; I promised and I've gone and messed up. Again!

"Please answer me, Liberty!" he shouts, "and tell me just what you think you're doing in here?"

I try to speak but my mouth won't work. I just stare at him, waiting for something to happen.

"Liberty," he persists, "I demand an explanation! Right now!"

"I… I… I…" I stutter. "I found the CD in the bookshelf last night, Daddy, and I didn't mean any harm… I just…"

"Just what, Liberty?" he boils. "Just what? Just thought you'd help yourself to my room and put your grubby mitts all over my things, did you?" He lunges towards me, trying to grab me.

"Daddy," I scream, pulling away. "Daddy, don't hurt me!"

"I'm not going to hurt you," he shouts, pulling at the purple dress, "I just want you to take that dress off! Now! It's not yours, Liberty!"

I pull at the dress. It's hard to get it over my head fast enough and I'm pulling and my dad's pulling and then a terrible tearing sound splits the air. We both gasp. The CD is playing on and on but my dad and I are frozen in time. I'm stuck. I can't stay like this for ever but if I move just one millimetre more I know the dress will tear again.

"I'm stuck," I say. I'm shaking all over and not knowing what to do. "I'm sorry, Daddy."

And I should have known that sorry was the worst thing ever to say, because he just whooshed it up in flames again.

"It's always sorry, with you, Liberty. Sorry! Sorry! Sorry! Is that the only word you know? I was beginning to think you'd improved lately, that we'd got over the teething problems. We were learning to get on fine together. But no, you have to push and push and push, just like your mother. Well, this is one push too far, young lady."

I can't breathe properly because the dress is half over my face and my arms are stuck in the air and beginning to feel tired. I try a little wriggle to see if I can set myself free, but I can feel that the fabric pulling and know it's about to tear.

"I need your help, Daddy," I say. "Please, I don't want to tear it any more."

He sighs, he's fuming mad, but when his hands touch the fabric of the dress, like magic, his anger dissolves into a puddle of tears. He crumples the dress to his face and breathes it in, urgently searching for something that might be left of my mum. He sniffs and sniffs, hoping. But it smells of musty old attics and cardboard boxes. He starts weeping and weeping into the purple and silver threads and then collapses on the bed, still clinging to the hem. He's trembling because all of the sadness that's been trapped inside him for years is escaping like air from a punctured balloon. He's left soggy and wrinkled. I'm about to topple over. I can't balance any more with him hanging on to the dress.

"Daddy," I whisper, "please help?"

Carefully, as if he were handling a newborn baby or a puppy, my dad manoeuvres the dress over my head and slips it away from my arms. He pulls it on to his lap, nursing it, stroking it, loving it like a long-lost friend. His eyes glaze over and he's staring into space, gently rocking backwards and forwards. I scuffle around getting myself back into my clothes, trying to cover myself up, trying to get rid of the bad feeling that is clinging to my skin. I eject the CD, put it back in its case and start putting all the things gently back in the trunk.

"Lissy," he cries. "Oh, Lissy. My Lissy." He curls up in a ball on the bed, cradling the purple dress and repeating her name over and over and over again.

I'm full of a million questions that are stomping around inside me, wanting answers, *right now!* I've had enough of being lied to; I've had enough of not knowing anything about my past. But I know I have to be careful not to set him off again. He's become a bomb on the bed that at any moment might explode in my face. I climb on the bed next to him and slowly, carefully, rest my hand on his shoulder. I can't remember the last time I touched my dad like this. His shoulder feels warm and for the first time ever, he doesn't shrug me off, instead he moves closer towards me, like a kitten looking for strokes. His tears dry up a little and just when I think he's feeling better, he starts whimpering my mum's name again and another huge wave of sadness crashes down over him and washes him away.

"Talk to me, Daddy," I whisper. "There's so much I need to know."

He sniffs, rubs his eyes and stares up at me. "I know, Libby," he says, "I know."

"Shall I get us both a coffee?" I ask.

He nods and while I'm making the coffee and finding a packet of our favourite biscuits, I hear him shuffling around in the bedroom, searching through the CDs. I feel strange inside. I feel like a heavy oak door with a thousand locks on it has been in the way of me finding out the truth about my life, and now my dad is about to open the door and let me go through to the other side. It's like I've been walking in fog for my whole life and now it's cleared and I can suddenly see the garden in front of me and I wonder if I'll be different when I know. I'm not feeling excited, I feel more serious, wondering what stories are about to hit my ears. I quickly text Cali and tell her I'm feeling too poorly to visit the old people today. I don't want her to suddenly barge in on the most important thing that's ever happened in my life and drag me off to vacuum someone old person's sitting room.

When I get back to the bedroom my dad has put on some music and is waiting on the bed, still clutching the purple dress. I hand him his coffee, he takes a sip and begins.

"What do you need to know?" he asks.

"Everything," I whisper, moving closer to him. "Like... is it true that you play the violin as well as my mum?"

He nods. "It is true."

"Then why did you stop?"

He groans. "Oh, Libby," he says, stroking my cheek, "it's such a long, long story."

"I've got all afternoon," I say, edging closer still, "I've cancelled the old people, so there's no hurry. Start from the beginning."

"I loved your mother so much, Libby," he sighs. "We met when we were young and fell in love over Bach and Tchaikovsky and Mozart and Vivaldi and all of the great composers of the world. We lived for our music. We lived, ate, slept and drowned in it. Music was our life. Your mother was much better than me; of course, I was never going to go as far as her, she was the one with the real talent. It came effortlessly to her; playing the violin was as easy as talking. Then Sebastian came along and it got more difficult to manage our careers and our family life, but your mother wouldn't give up. She was just like you Liberty, she'd push and push and push until she got what she needed. She'd never give up or compromise. But someone needed to be here for Sebastian, so I stayed at home while your mother travelled the world and became more and more famous and more and more in demand."

He sips his coffee and stares into the distance, like he's waiting for the right words to drop into his mouth. I slide a little closer. We're leaning back on a pile of pillows and our arms are touching. I've never sat so close to my dad before. He smiles at me and shakes out the purple dress and lays it across both our laps to keep us warm. I don't say one word because I don't want to break this spell.

"And then you came along," he smiles, stroking my hair from my eyes. "Liberty, my darling girl. You were so beautiful, Libby, so small and perfect and delicate. It would have been impossible to cart two babies around the world going from concert tour to concert tour so I stopped the travelling completely and decided to play for pleasure only. I stayed at home and cared for the two of you. And I begged your mother to stay too. You needed her, you both did. But she got into such a frenzy with it all she just couldn't stop. Music was like breath to her, you see and without it she thought that she might just fade away and die."

And then his voice cracks and he starts crying again and little waves of tears break over him. I start crying too and gently he lifts his arm, wraps it around me and pulls me in close. I'm breathless and I'm not really crying for my mum, more for all the time that I've lost with my dad, more for all the moments that we haven't shared like this. In all my memory my dad has never held me like this before; we have never been so close.

"And you see," he continues, "if only I hadn't begged her, if only I'd just let her be, then none of this would ever have happened."

I take hold of his hand to let him know that I'm here for him, to let him know that if he carries on with the difficult part of the story, I'm not going to slide away and fall off of the edge of the world.

Chapter 30

I squeeze his hand...

We're both quiet for a moment, listening to the violin sounds flying out of the laptop and soaring towards the sky. Sometimes it takes time to find the right words to tell somebody something that might be difficult for them to hear. And I've waited the whole of my life, so there's no hurry now.

My dad sighs.

"She was on her way to the airport," he says, "she was flying to Japan for a big series of concerts. She'd asked me to take her but Sebastian was so upset because he didn't want Mummy to go away again, I thought it would be better for everyone if she went in a taxi. I'd been begging and begging her not to go. She was going to be away for three whole months, touring around, and I just couldn't bear to be apart from her for that long again and you were so tiny, and… and… and I was so angry, I didn't want to make it easy for her to go."

I squeeze his hand.

"So she left with us shouting at each other and with Sebastian crying and you squawking for a feed. Then the next thing I knew, two police officers knocked at the door, came into the house, sat me down and started making me coffee. I was bemused. I didn't really know what was going on. Then they told me that a huge lorry had appeared from nowhere and jack-knifed in front of Mummy's taxi, killing her and the driver on impact. I couldn't quite take it all in. Sebastian needed his tea and you had a nappy-full and I just had to get on with it all. There was no one else to do it. For days I just moved from breakfast to lunch, from lunch to dinner. From getting you both up, to filling our day and getting you both back to bed. Your granny helped for a while but eventually she got on my nerves. She told me I should keep your mother alive in the house and tell you as you were growing up exactly what had happened. But I couldn't, Libby, I was too scared, the whole thing was just too painful. There was no room for anything else but the day-to-day chores and getting us fed and nothing else really mattered any more. Your mother didn't stand a chance, Libby. And if only I hadn't been so stubborn, she might still have been here with us today. It was all my fault."

A huge invisible hand swoops down, crumples my dad up like a sheet of useless paper, and collapses him on my lap. His tears come again and now they don't scare me. I understand. It's like they've been waiting somewhere inside him, in the same place as this terrible secret, waiting and waiting to be freed. We stay like this for ages, until my dad's tears ebb away. I'm not crying. Now I know the truth, I feel like a butterfly set free. Everything is beginning to make sense.

Suddenly my dad jumps up and picks up the pink photo album with my name on and runs his hand through his bed-head hair.

"I made this for you," he says, handing it to me. "I stuck the sequins on and filled it with pictures of you until the very last page. Then something snapped in me, Libby, I was only just holding things together for us and I knew something had to change. I was getting too maudlin with it all, it wasn't good for any of us. I had to shake things up."

I flip through the album feeling different about it now. It was my dad who made it, not my mum! A soft warm glow grows in my tummy.

"So you did love me then?" I whisper, stroking the photo of us both on my first birthday.

"Love you!" he roars. "Liberty, I adored you. I adored the very ground you crawled on. I adored every tiny bit of you. You were so delicious I had to stop myself from eating you up!"

I giggle.

"So what happened?" I brave.

"Oh, I don't know," he says, pulling me to my feet and leading me to the kitchen where he starts preparing lunch. "I tried so hard but it all went wrong. I couldn't seem to make the place happy like she did. Something was missing, like a gap I couldn't fill. I thought it was best to cut us off from your mother's side of the family because having them around was too painful for us all. Too many redheads in one room, you see. And then the more you grew, the more like her you became. It's incredible, Libby, how alike you are. Just looking at you tore at every painful memory and every bitter regret. I loved her so much; missing her was like torture. And then you started up with the whole music thing. As a toddler you'd dance and jiggle and tap and then you went on about those darned violin lessons when you were seven. I just couldn't bear to see history repeat itself. I couldn't bear to see you become so obsessed that you ruined your own life too."

I pour us some juice; it's weird listening to my dad talk like this.

"So I did a terrible thing," he sighs, getting out the plates. "I thought I could control you, Liberty. I thought if I just cut music out of our lives then I could guide you in another direction and keep you safe. And the music was too painful for me to hear, it reminded me of her, it reminded me of everything I'd left behind. I had to rid us of it. So I locked all the memories away in the trunks, banned music from the house, refused to talk about the past and bit by bit we started to build a new life. Your granny fought hard with me, but in the end I had my own way. That's why we can't stand being around each other any more."

I don't feel very hungry but I sit at the table anyway

and pick at my food. An anger bubble is pushing its way up. I try to keep it down because I can't risk it; I need to hear the whole of this story, first. We need to set things straight.

"But starting a new life was hard, Libby. I had no experience in anything but music and being a dad. So I took all the money your mother had made, and there was plenty of it, and ploughed it into a business. But the business took me away from you and then the further away I got, the easier it became to keep my hurt at bay. And then with the credit crunch I went and lost all the money and opened all the trunks and discovered that all the hurt and all the pain hadn't gone away at all. It was still there, just as fresh, waiting to leap out and bite me."

I'm listening to my dad, but I can't stop thinking about the violin on his bed that first morning we arrived here. I know it's somewhere, hidden in this secret, waiting to come out and be played.

"Did my mum love me?" I whisper.

"Of course she did," he says, stroking my cheek. "She adored you, Libby, and Sebastian. But the music was like an addiction to her, she couldn't get enough of it. She didn't know when to stop. I will understand if you can't forgive me, Libby. What I did was wrong, I know that now."

"I know that feeling of music being as important as breathing," I say.

He sits up straight, suddenly alert. "You do?"

I nod. My angry words are bubbling up to the surface but I have to be careful here. I have to tell him gently.

"I need music, Daddy, just like my mum. It's a part of me, I can't help it and you have to stop controlling me. You have to let me be myself. I might get to be a success, like you want me to be, if you'd let me do things my way. I promise I won't get hurt. I promise I won't hurt anybody else and I promise you won't lose me."

He nods, holds both my hands in his and drops his head.

"I know I have to let you be you. I know what I did was unfair. I'm sorry, sweetheart. I tried my best but I truly messed up, didn't I? And so much for the big success, look at me! I'm ruined in every way!"

And then I don't know why, but we both start giggling. We're gazing into each other's eyes and the giggles just keep on coming.

"I'm such an idiot," he giggles.

"You are," I smile.

Then he pulls me up and folds me into his arms. I feel warm all over. We're here, just my dad and me, together.

Chapter 31

If you want to come, that is...

"Oh, there's just one more confession," he says, leading me back to his room.

He heaves the old, brown, sticker-covered suitcase onto the bed and rummages in his pocket for the key. My heart is beating like a balloon full of birds. I wish, I wish, I wish. I hope, I hope, I hope.

"I had to lock them away," he says, "it's the only thing I could do to stop myself playing. You see, I know that feeling of music being as important as breathing too. We all have the family bug," he smiles. "Except Sebastian, of course, he's the only sensible one out of all of us."

He opens the case and lying inside is not one violin case, but two!

"One each," he smiles, looking like a huge shadow of shame has been lifted from his face.

"This is for you," he says, handing me the same dusty case that I drew the heart on. "It was your mother's, of course."

My hands are shaking as I open the catches. Lying inside a beautiful red velvet nest is my mum's shiny violin, untouched by time or tears or death. I pull it out. I'm shaking all over and my breathing is rapid; I'm nervous now, I have to do this right. I pull out the bow, apply the rosin to the hair and tighten it so it's ready to play. Then carefully, I pick up the violin, place it under my chin and play. The bow kisses the strings like long-lost friends meeting for the first time in years. They stroke each other and their out-of-tune sounds fill the room with an eerie wail. I laugh and my dad laughs then I tune up so I can play properly and I play a tune I know by heart. My dad is watching me; I can feel his eyes looking and looking, checking what I'm doing. I feel nervous and shy. Then he starts moving quietly around me. Adjusting my elbow, relaxing my shoulder, shifting my legs.

"There…" he says, gently coaching me, and, "just like that… yes… good girl… a little more like that… yes… lift your elbow…"

When he's got me in the right position, he sits back on the bed to watch and when I've finished, he applauds.

"You're a natural, Libby," he smiles. "There's no doubt about it, you really have got the family bug and I feel embarrassed that I've kept you from it for so long. But to be fair, you've a lot of catching up to do. I'm not sure where we'll get the cash from, but with the right lessons and enough commitment to practice… well maybe… you just might make it… I think it's possible."

My eyes are glittering with joy. My heart is about to burst open, letting a thousand sunflowers and roses peep their beautiful heads out and climb towards the sun. He's saying I can have lessons and I haven't even had to ask! But there's another question bouncing on my tongue, burning in my tummy. Would it be too greedy, I wonder, to ask for something else?

"Can I?" I stutter, "Please… just…"

"Spit it out," he says. "Don't be scared. Let's face it,

after all I've confessed to you today, Libby, nothing can be worse than that."

The question is pushing through my lips, wanting to pop out, but a part of me is holding it back. I'm scared to ask, I'm not used to asking for anything. Ooh, I don't know! Can I? Will I look stupid? I don't even have anything to wear!

"Come on, come on," he says, "spit it out, I'm itching to play."

"I just wondered… if I could… I mean… if you'd let me play the little violin part in *Bugsy Malone*?"

"What are you talking about, Liberty? I'm lost."

"Well," I say, "don't you remember, on my birthday how they all started talking about *Bugsy Malone*? And we had the big argument and I told you I wanted play and then I ran off and Tyler brought me home? Well, I asked at the school and Mrs O said they didn't have an instrument…"

And the whole story comes tumbling out, like an avalanche down a mountain.

"Have you got the music?"

I nod.

"Well, what are you waiting for?"

I charge into my room, pull the music out from under my mattress, hug it tightly in my arms and skip back into my dad's room. We tune our instruments and then my dad starts teaching me the piece. I can't believe what's happening! It's not too difficult because I taught myself the tune on the school keyboard, but he's making sure I get it right. He's fussing about my posture and picking holes in my technique, but I don't care. I want him to show me, I want us to play together. I learn the piece fast, then he takes the music away and we play it together, over and over until I've learned it by heart. We keep on catching each other's eyes and laughing and giggling with the madness of it all.

"I'm impressed, Libby," he says, smiling, "really."

While I'm showering and getting ready to race off to school to find Mrs O, the sound of my dad playing his own violin fills our flat with music, air and glittering light. We can both breathe again, at last. Everything has suddenly come alive, like someone has picked some fresh, bright daffodils and filled our flat with their blooms. And suddenly I can't wait to phone Alice and tell her. And Cali and Dylan are going to be amazed and even Tyler and Joyce and all the other old people.

"Got everything you need?" says my dad, helping me into my coat.

And then I suddenly realise that I can't go because I don't have anything to wear. I slump on my dad's bed.

"It doesn't matter," I say, holding back my tears, "it's not the end of the world, not compared with everything else today."

"What do you need?" he says.

"I guess some black trousers would do. I could use my school ones," I say. "Then I'd need a white shirt and a black bow tie."

"Well that's easy," he says, searching through the trunk mess, "you can use these."

My dad hands me his very own concert clothes that were hiding away with my mum's dresses. I can't believe he'd let me wear them.

"I can't," I say. "They're your precious things, your memories."

"Oh, poppycock," he smiles. "If there's one thing I've learned today, Libby, it's to live in the present. What's the use of hiding these old memories away? It won't bring her back, will it? It won't change anything. Take them, go on, and have fun."

I didn't know the word fun was in my dad's brain dictionary.

"It starts at 7pm," I say, rushing from our flat with my violin and his clothes in my hand, "if you want to come, that is."

Chapter 32

Bugsy is *brilliant*...

When I get to school the drama studio is quiet and dark. So much has happened this afternoon. There's so much to take in and so many questions that I still have to ask and I feel dizzy with it all. I feel different about my dad, too. I hate that he's been so angry with me for so long, but now I know the reasons why I can just about begin to understand. I mean, I must remember that *he* was the one who stayed with Sebastian and me, while *she* got lost in her music. *He* was the one who gave up playing in concerts to look after us, while *she* travelled all over the world. And all this time I've been thinking that life would be better if my *mum* were still around, when really it was my *dad* who was always trying his best. I want to run and say sorry for hating him for so long and I want to tell him that I forgive him for everything, because although he did do a pretty terrible job at it, he did, at least, try his best. He did what he thought was right at the time.

I can't actually believe that I'm sitting here, waiting for *Bugsy Malone* to begin. I feel silly and a bit embarrassed. Mrs O's going to think I'm mad for turning up like this and although it might seem strange, actually playing in *Bugsy Malone* suddenly doesn't feel so very important any more. I mean I have my whole life to play the violin, what's so special about today? I can hear people coming into the school. Cali is singing, 'I'm Feeling Fine', at the top of her voice and if I had supersonic hearing, I know I'd hear Dylan cracking his knuckles. I can hear Mr Forrest's voice telling everyone to calm down and Mrs O directing the orchestra towards the studio. And suddenly I realise that I'm feeling fine too and that I don't really need to be here doing this. I mean playing in *Bugsy* will be great but there really are more important thing in life, like finding out about your past for instance and getting to know your dad when he's suddenly changed from being an angry monster into a totally new man that you never thought would exist.

And I can't wait to see what our lives are going to be like now. I mean I know that miracles don't happen overnight, but just imagine what it would be like going to a real live classical concert with him, or even having music playing on the radio in our flat. I'm just about to duck out of the way and make my escape through a side door when Cali bursts into the room.

"Liberty!" she smiles, doing a Bugsy dance across the floor to get to me. "What are you doing here? I thought you were ill."

"It's a long story," I say. "I'll tell you about it one day, but basically I took your advice, Cali, and I found out all about my mum. And look," I smile, holding my violin in the air, "I got this too, it was my mum's."

"Does that mean you're playing in *Bugsy*?" she squeals.

I nod and Mrs O and Mr Forrest clap out loud.

"I had every faith in you, Liberty," smiles Mrs O. "I knew you'd get something together."

"Come, come, ladies," sings Mr Forrest, "there's work to be done, and fast!"

So, quickly they run me through my part, showing which side of the stage I have to come on, how I have to walk around the restaurant tables, and when I have to leave. In the changing room everyone's going mad with excitement. We're all getting dressed up and putting our stage make-up on and having fun practicing singing and dancing. I never thought I'd be part of this. And it's amazing to be here, but there's something else, nibbling away at me, and with me, when something starts to nibble, I just can't let it go. Just like my mum, I suppose.

Just before *Bugsy* starts I hide in the wings and look out to the audience to see if my dad has arrived.

"Quick," I call to Cali, "you just have to look at this."

And there on the front row is my dad and Hanna and Joyce and Jean and Len and Ivor. I can't believe it! They've all come to see us! Everyone is here! Then I see Tyler arrive and I can't believe my eyes. Tyler in the theatre! He squeezes in next to my dad and smiles. Hanna's handing sweets around and my dad has a camera ready in his hand.

When it's my turn to go on stage, I suddenly feel scared. I've never played in public before and I'm afraid I might mess things up. But once I'm there, under the warm lights, looking out at a sea of faces, I relax. I was born to perform, I remind myself. Go girl. And here I am totally swimming in love. Everyone's here to see me and I have my dad's precious shirt on my back and his tie around my neck and I know they'll bring me good luck. I gaze up to the roof and imagine myself seeing right through it and out to the glittering blanket of stars that are twinkling overhead, and I know my mum is there too, wrapped up in them, watching me, cheering me on.

Bugsy is brilliant! I'm brilliant, Cali is brilliant and even Dylan gets a laugh with his brilliant knuckle crunching. I never knew happiness like this was possible and I have to pinch myself to make sure I've not got stuck in a dream.

After the show we all pile back to Hanna's for a party. She's made a mountain of food and decorated the flat like Hollywood. She found an old piece of red carpet at the dump and cut a strip off it, so it's like the real red carpet that the stars walk down to collect their Oscars. Everyone takes turns in walking down the carpet and everyone cheers and makes a fuss and takes photos like the paparazzi do. And of course, Hanna being Hanna, she's got an Oscar for us all, even for me.

"But you didn't even know I was going to be in *Bugsy*," I say.

"I always have an Oscar up my sleeve, Liberty," she smiles, "for you never know when you're going to bump into a real-life star."

On the way back down to our flat, I slip my hand into my dad's. He holds me tight and smiles.

Chapter 33

Me glorious me...

So much has happened since *Bugsy*. Sebastian's home for Christmas and Hanna's arranged a massive Christmas meal for us and her family and all of the old people, to have in the community office near the canal. Tyler and his mum and brothers and sister are joining us too and believe it or not, Sebastian and Tyler are actually getting on quite well, even though they're so different. And now we're allowed music in our flat they're downloading it together all of the time. Tyler's deadly serious about doing that college course to be a youth worker person and Sebastian's helping him with his application forms so he can start in September. And Sebastian is still brilliant and has got into Cambridge

University to study something important, but I can't remember what.

"I've gotta get myself out of this dump, one day," says Tyler. "The rate I was going I'd have been in prison before I reached eighteen. So I'll opt for the education route, me thinks."

Mr Forrest was so impressed with Cali in *Bugsy Malone* that he's promised to do another musical soon and he says that when she's older, he'll coach her so she can get into drama school. And I don't need to tell you what she said to that, except for the fact that it starts with, "Holly…" and ends with, "… here I come!"

Dylan has gone off drama and is getting more interested in music, like me, and he's planning to make a band and become a famous pop star.

My dad and Hanna have got the Community Action Scheme off the ground and have managed to get the funding for them both to have a job. But Alice's dad has offered my dad a full-time job with his company, so I've told him he needs to put his head down and pull his socks up and make a decision pretty soon.

I've got a bit of thinking to do too. Once my granny in Scotland discovered about my dad and the credit crunch and that I'd been taken away from my old school, she went bananas. She started getting busy with things and interfering, as usual and is insisting that my life will be in ruins if I don't go back to my old school. She's going to sell some shares to fund my education until my dad gets back on his feet. I'm not sure though. I loved my old school, but I also love it here. Dad says I have until the end of the Christmas holidays to make up my mind. But the brilliant thing is my dad and granny are actually on speaking terms again. She's happy that the secret about what happened to my mum has come out at last and is very happy that she proved my dad's theory wrong.

"I told you, Henry," she said, when they were speaking on the telephone, "nothing good comes of keeping secrets. There's no shame in life, so long as we can bring it out in the open and say what needs to be said."

And of course she's delighted that my dad's taken up the violin again. She knows he's doing it just for fun, but she's glad for him all the same.

Sebastian is pleased about the secret coming out too and he and I spent an afternoon pinning pictures of our mum all over our flat. And he cut one up small and slipped it into his brown leather wallet. Yesterday, when we were all lying about the place getting into the Christmas spirit, my dad got out his violin and played the tune my mum used to play Sebastian when he was falling asleep. I watched him close his eyes to listen and saw the music reach deep inside of him to a soft place where he could remember her.

I've made up with Alice, because best friends always do, and she's overexcited to the stars and back about the possibility of me coming back to school. But of course, Cali and Hanna and Dylan and Tyler and all the old people want me to stay here.

"Spoilt for choice, you are," smiles my dad. "But remember that this time, Liberty, the choice is yours. It's your life and I finally understand that I can't live it for you; you have to do what's right for you."

Oh, yes, and I found out from Mrs Cobb more about our school motto and those Latin words mean: *Success is not what you achieve, it is who you are*. And I'm excited to be discovering more about who I am every single day. At midnight on New Year's Eve, I'm going to make a resolution to keep on being *ME GLORIOUS ME* for the rest of my precious, precious, life.

Chapter 34

Like glitter on my smile...

It's Christmas Eve. My dad is watching an old movie on the telly, Sebastian is out with Tyler and I should be going to bed, but I can't. The thing that started nibbling away on *Bugsy Malone* day has stopped nibbling and is now biting great chunks out of my brain.

"There's something I really need to do, Daddy," I say, "and it can't wait any longer."

"Oh, dear," he smiles, "I can smell trouble. Tell me, Liberty, what is it now?"

"I have to go to her grave, Daddy, please? I have to see it with my very own eyes. I have to take her some flowers and play her a tune and let her know I'm OK and that I love her, because now I understand everything."

"Are you sure?"

I nod. So, we leave a note for Sebastian, pick up our violins and slip away into the night in our crusty old car. We stop at the petrol station and buy some pink carnations on special offer. It feels a bit strange getting special offer ones when we should be getting much more amazing ones, especially when I've never even seen my mum's grave before. I can tell my dad feels the same by the way he's frantically counting out the change making sure he's got enough money in his wallet. But I don't think my mum will mind, she'll understand. She's had so many Christmases alone without us visiting that I think she'd even be happy if we arrived without any flowers at all. When we get to the graveyard it's dark and the gate is padlocked shut.

"Don't worry," says my dad, grabbing a huge torch from the boot of the car, "I know a secret route in. I come here a lot, you know, just to talk and be with your mother."

We walk along the road, scramble through some bushes and my dad heaves me over the fence and climbs over after me. We're giggling again. I mean, who on earth breaks into a cemetery in the middle of the night with their dad, to see their mum and play the violin? We walk past hundreds of sleeping graves. Some have angels standing over them and some have flowers bunched in jam-jars making them look bright. All of them have writing on the headstone saying things about who the person was and who they're leaving behind. I can't really read them in the dark, but I'd like to come back in the daytime one day, because some of them look so old they might even have been here since Charles Dickens's day.

"I did like the Charles Dickens books, really," I say, taking my dad's hand. "I was just cross, that's all. And I do forgive you, Daddy. I do. None of it was your fault, you know."

We walk the rest of the way in silence and my heart starts pounding in my chest when my dad points out my mum's grave to me. I know she's not really here any more; well, apart from her body that is, or her bones at least. But it feels like *she's* really here too, like she's really with us, close by. It's almost like if I reached out I might be able to find her in the dark. I take the torch from my dad and shine it on her headstone. There are hundreds of music notes carved in the white stone that are playing themselves high up to the sky. My mum's special words read:

Lissy Parfitt 1965–1999. Our glittering success. Play music with the angels darling and wrap yourself in stars. Loving you always, Henry, Sebastian and Liberty.

I trace the word Lissy with my finger, my mummy, my mummy. I don't feel sad really, more curious. There's so much more I need to know.

"Was Sebastian named after Johann Sebastian Bach?" I ask.

"Ooh, you're quick," my dad smiles. "Yes, he was."

"And me?"

"Ooh, you," he laughs, taking out his violin, "well, we discovered that your mother was pregnant with you when we were in New York. So you know, the Statue of Liberty, it seemed the best choice. And you certainly live up to your name, child!"

"One more question for tonight?" I giggle.

"Ooh, go on then, just one more."

"When can I meet her family?"

Then my dad turns into a pretend growling bear and chases me around and around my mum's grave, laughing and laughing and I'm squealing with happiness.

"What are we going to play then?" he asks.

"Bugsy?" I giggle.

And here we are standing in a dark graveyard somewhere in London on Christmas Eve, in a supposedly serious place, near my mum's grave, playing the tune from *Bugsy Malone*. We're standing opposite each other and our violin sounds are dancing through the air, swirling with the angels, zooming up to the moon and shooting with the stars.

"So beautiful… you are so like your mother… I'm so proud of you, Liberty," he sighs.

And at that moment his heart pops out a little gift-wrapped parcel of love that lands like glitter on my smile.

Acknowledgements

Thank you Daniel – my wonderful I.T. support man, personal chef, foot masseur, hottie maker, lover, husband and friend for your presence and your love throughout the entire process of creating *Glitter*.

Thank you my gorgeous children – I'm so inspired by you all; Jane with your effortless gift of sprinkling glittering love and joy in such abundance through my days; Tim with your tender-hearted wisdom and astonishing depth; Sam with your courageous commitment to living your truth; Joe with your continued interest, support and encouragement in my work and tenacious passion for your own and Ben with your open-hearted expression and your cheeky, winning smile. I'm so touched to be part of your lives.

Thank you my wonderful sister Susie, for your constancy and for your truly unconditional love. Thank you my lovely brother Tim, for your quietly constant love. Thank you my lovely friend Dawne, for our deeply enriching friendship, which means so much to me. Thank you Paul, for always believing in me, always loving me.

Thank you my fantastic readers: Alice, Claire and Darcey. Thank you Thea, Matt and Year 7 Writhlington School for allowing me to join your drama and music lessons. Thank you Jayne, for your research and support and Fifi Fiddle, for violin info.

Thank you a million times over wonderful Eve, my agent, for believing in me and for all your support, care and loveliness. And thank you wonderful Rachel, my editor, for guiding me so tenderly through the whole process of bringing *Glitter* into being. So blessed am I! Thank you Rose, Kate, Tom, Hannah, Catherine, Heike and everyone else from HarperCollins, for all your hard work and enthusiasm. Thank you Dave, and the rest of the Punktillio crew, for your fan page support and for your patience in dealing with a mad woman like me! And thank you to all the people who I'll probably never get to meet – those who plant and cut the sustainable forests, make the paper, print the pages, wrap and pack and drive and stack and sell my books – without all of you *Glitter* would be left drifting in my imagination instead of being read by the world.

Thank you Adam – words can't express my gratitude – but then you're dyslexic so I guess words don't matter so much! But gratitude is here.

I feel so touched by life. xxx

MORE AMAZING
READS FROM
Kate Maryon

*"We talk about everything. Dad and me. About all
the mysteries inside of us. About all our wonderings
of the world. But tomorrow my dad goes to war.
Then what will I do?"*

Jemima's dad is in the Army and he's off to
Afghanistan for six whole months. Her mum's about
to have another baby and Gran's head is filled with
her own wartime memories. So while Mima is
sending Dad millions of guardian angels to keep
him safe, who is looking out for her?

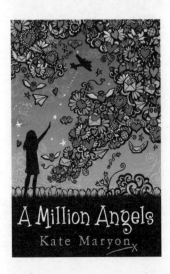

*"The page is staring at me waiting for words, but I don't
even know where to start. I'd quite like
to begin the letter with something like,
Dear Mum, Thanks for ruining my life,
but I don't think that's the kind of letter that
Auntie Cass has in mind."*

Tiff's sparkling world comes crashing down when
her mum commits a crime. Packed off to live with
family in the dullest place on the planet – and without
Mum around – everything seems to
lose its shine . . .

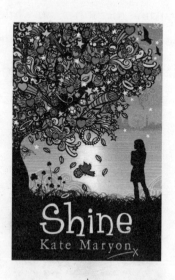